Alastair Hunter
23/11/69

Strange Tales of the
Western Isles

To my dearest daughter
Molly

Strange Tales of the Western Isles

By
Halbert J. Boyd
Author of " Reprieve," " Men and Marvels," etc.

Eneas Mackay
Stirling

First published 1930

Printed in Scotland

Contents

Strange Tales of the Western Isles

Foreword

To the few readers who will glance at a preface to a book of short stories such as this, I would address a word or two of explanation as to how these tales came to be written. Though my remote ancestors were of Celtic stock, I can claim no Highland origin, and, therefore, it may seem almost an impertinence on the part of a Sassenach, such as I, to attempt an interpretation of the spirit and character of the Highlands; nor can I claim either knowledge of its language, or any profound study of its history. I had not even explored its territory until little over a year ago when private affairs called me, about that time, within easy reach of these regions, and at once I was caught by the marvellous magnetism of their spell. Though railway trains and motor cars with their hordes of tourists have penetrated almost to the remotest parts, they have not wholly marred the majesty and grandeur of these hills and glens, nor have they quite banished the spirit of romance which yet lingers there. But a summer month spent in the Hebrides convinced me that in these islands only—less accessible to the visitor, as they are, than is the mainland—customs and beliefs, once prevalent throughout the whole area of the Gaelic speaking race, still linger in secret. Superstitions are still whispered there; belief in the supernatural, while openly scoffed at, is covertly held. The story of the dreaded water-horse which, as legend tells, was wont to arise from the lonely loch in human form captivating, but destructive particularly to womankind, may be laughed at by the fireside, but no young girl will choose to pass alone by that loch at night. The knoll which those of old declared to be haunted by the fairies—that dangerous and malicious race— or by the glaistig—half woman, half fiend—will be traversed without tremor in the sunlight; but not after twilight or dusk has fallen.

Whence came these strange beliefs? And to what extent did they influence the lives of those who held them in entirety? These questions arise readily to the mind, and it was in my endeavour to find the answers to them that I became possessed of various books dealing with the subjects of Highland legend and superstition. Of these books those written by the late Rev. J. G. Campbell have seemed to me by far the best. They are almost all out of print and some are exceedingly difficult to procure; but by great good fortune I was able to buy some and to borrow others.

In most of the following stories I have taken as a theme one or another of these Highland superstitions and around it have grouped imaginary characters, in order to illustrate that belief in operation. In

Foreword

some, such as " Thyra," " The Black Dog of Macphie," and " The Black Raven of Glengarry," I have retold genuine legends ; but, I must confess, often to have taken very great liberty in the way of alteration and addition. In the Appendix I endeavour to atone for these misdeeds by giving intact either the original legend, or its summary.

HALBERT J. BOYD.

GLASGOW, 1930.

THE BLACK DOG OF MACPHIE.

MACPHIE, laird of Colonsay, set forth one October morning for the hills. He carried powder flask, shot belt and gun, for his intention was to shoot the moor-fowl. He went alone, without even a dog, because that which had usually followed him on such occasions had died the previous day, and, but for his sixteen foster-brothers, there were not many men who sought his companionship. For strange tales were told of the laird, whispered on black winter nights around the peat fires, or in the summer gloaming as women span at the sheiling doors. Not quite canny was Macphie, if all stories were true. It was suspected that Mac-Vic-Allan, lord of Moidart, could have told the truth about the laird if he had so chosen; for did not folk say that Macphie had been his guest when they were confronted by an elle-maid who had claimed the laird as her former lover? Only by hounding on his dogs, which all fairy folk abhor, had she been driven at length from the point of Arasaig. No, Macphie of Colonsay was not a man with whom to wander when the mist lay on the hills, and stray winds whispered through the bracken, or whirled in sudden elfin eddies through the glen.

So the laird on this October afternoon was unaccompanied as he hunted on the hills. The day had been bright when he set forth ; but the wind, veering to the south west, had blown up heavy clouds, and drifting mist and rain obscured the view as evening fell. A tired and disappointed man was Macphie long ere then. Little success had rewarded his efforts ; whether it was that the rain had damped the priming of his fowling-piece, or that a forgetful ghillie calling after him as he had set forth, had brought bad luck to him, as such ill-omened practice was bound to do, he could not tell ; the fact remained that again and again his gun had misfired, and even when discharged, his aim had often been untrue. But worse was to befall him : so thick hung the mist that, well though he knew every glen and knoll of the neighbourhood, he lost his way. Like a dripping blanket the heavy clouds clung around him. Heather and bracken streamed cataracts of moisture on him as he brushed past. Not a sound was to be heard, no ripple or splash of river or burn which might have served as guide. Pulling his bonnet over his brows, and wrapping his saturated plaid closer around him he plunged

doggedly on, raging to think of the blazing
fire, the fragrantly steaming cauldron of
mutton broth, which, as supper, must be awaiting him at home, not many miles distant; and
yet a hungry night, spent beneath the shelter
of a rock, seemed his only prospect.

Almost he had resigned himself to this
apparently inevitable fate, when suddenly
filtering through the gloom, a faint light was
discernable, and, next moment, the laird
found himself standing before a rude, thatched
cabin. A small unglazed window was before
him, and peering in he saw a single chamber,
destitute of furniture, saving for one broken
wooden bench. In the centre of the earthen
floor a few peats and faggots burned, sending
upward a column of smoke to escape from a
hole in the roof. On one side was piled a
great heap of dried bracken, and on the other
crouched an old, grey-bearded man, slowly
stirring a pot which stood upon the embers.

Strange that Macphie, familiar though all
his people and his lands were to him, could
not remember ever previously to have seen
either this cottage or this old man. His
failure, however, by no means deterred him,
wet, tired, and hungry as he was. He therefore at once sought and found a crazy door,
and, without further delay or ceremony,
pushed it open and entered the dwelling.

B

"Good evening to you," Macphie addressed the old man, "and who might you be?"

"Who I am does not matter at all, but I know you very well, Macphie, and have been expecting you this night. You are very welcome." Saying which the old man arose, removing his bonnet courteously and motioning the laird to be seated.

"It is strange that you should have been expecting me, since I know neither you nor your house. I have lost my way."

"And yet you are not far from home. Will you be pleased to sit?"

Having seated the laird on the bench, the old man then removed the pot from the fire, poured out the water which the vessel contained, and laid before the laird a fresh salmon-trout which he urged his guest to eat. This Macphie did with relish, washing down the food with usquebaugh with which also his host supplied him.

Then warmed and fed Macphie looked around him and observed that in the heap of bracken on the other side of the fire lay a bitch, with two puppies, one brindled, one black.

"These are handsome puppies," he remarked.

"They are all that," answered the old man,

" and it is for you to choose which you would like to have."

" It is indeed a dog that I am wanting, and since you so politely offer me one I shall gladly accept your offer."

" Choose then," urged the old man.

Never before had Macphie seen more beautiful puppies ; but of the two the black seemed the more beautiful ; its coat was glossy as the black-cock's wing, and its eyes were intelligent and bright.

" It is the black puppy that I will be having," cried Macphie.

" Ah ! you do not choose well," the other warned.

" It is this one or none that I will have, however."

" Take then the black puppy since you are set on it, and care well for it, though there will be but the one day in which it will do service for you."

So Macphie took the puppy and enquired of the old man whether he could direct him to his own house as he was unwilling to pass the night in so poor an abode.

" That can I easily do," answered the other, and leading the laird to the door, gave him careful directions, promising that should these be followed he would be at home in less than half an hour.

The mist still clung closely as Macphie stepped out into the night ; yet hardly had he proceeded a gun shot, when the stars shone undimmed above, and, looking around, he at once recognized the glen about him. Yet never before, he felt sure, had he seen the hut from which he had just departed ; and though next day he revisited the spot where it must have stood, no trace of the dwelling was to be found, nor did he ever again meet the old grey-bearded man who had entertained him that night.

The black puppy, however, he took home, and there, as months passed, it grew into as fine a hound as any of the folk of Colonsay had ever seen. But try as he might, Macphie never succeeded in training it to the hunting. Only at times it would disappear for days together, until all would think it lost ; but always it returned. Whether it hunted by itself on these occasions none knew. Certainly no deer killed by it were ever found. But when Macphie or his foster-brothers set out for the hills, no persuasions, threats or blows would induce the hound to follow them.

" Shoot the useless brute, handsome though he be," the foster-brothers would urge.

" Not so," Macphie always answered, " the black dog's day will come yet."

Almost two years had passed, when one

morning Macphie called his foster-brothers
together and proposed that they should take
boat with him to the neighbouring island of
Jura and there spend a day in hunting. Now,
Jura at that time was uninhabited by men,
but had no equal as a hunting ground, for it
was full of deer and roe. Intent on his sport
Macphie had frequently visited it in the past,
and on such occasions he had been accustomed
to use as sleeping accommodation what was
known as the ' Big Cave '—a huge recess suitable in all respects for the purpose to which
it was put by him, in spite of the fact that in
the roof was a flaw sufficiently large to admit
the passage of a human body. This aperture
had, however, its use as an escape for the smoke
from any fire which the hunter might light
within the shelter.

To Jura, then, Macphie and his foster brothers
determined to go, their plan being to spend two
nights within the Big Cave, and to occupy
the intervening day with their sport. They
collected, therefore, bedclothing and provisions
sufficient for their use, and these, with guns
and ammunition, were loaded within a boat
ready for departure.

Just as they were about to leave the house,
one of the young men turned, and what should
he see but the black hound standing within,

watching them as if eager to be called—magnificent in glossy symmetry, ideal for the chase.

"Let us see," cried the young man, "whether he will come to-day; for surely a better dog to look upon there could never be."

So Macphie whistled and called to the hound and, to the delight of all, the animal obeyed, bounding towards them, while all awaited it. But suddenly it paused in its career, as suddenly as if arrested by an unseen hand, and stood rigid, nor could any persuasion or violence avail to renew its advance. They swore at it, they kicked it, but the dog shrank back, refusing to accompany them.

"Useless brute!" cried the young men. "Why do you not shoot it?"

"No," Macphie answered," the black dog's day has not come yet."

Without further delay the men clambered into the boat and, seizing the oars, pushed out from the land. But hardly had they done so when the sky which, until then, had been cloudless, was swiftly and darkly overcast, and a sudden, fierce wind arose and blew so tempestuously that the boat was in danger of being swamped. Only with the utmost difficulty and in peril of their lives were the hunters at length able to turn about their craft and make for the shore again. All that day the storm raged and only towards night-fall was calm restored.

Next morning, strange to say, the same experience befell them. Again, just as they were about to embark, the black dog was observed lingering near. Again they called it and again it refused to come. Once more Macphie, on the same pretext as before, resisted the advice given to him to destroy the hound ; and once more they were storm stayed.

On the third day as they prepared to set forth, nothing was seen of the hound, and no effort was made to find him. The men had again loaded their boat and were together hauling it from the shore when suddenly, swift as a thunderbolt, the hound bounded unbidden past them and sprang on board. In speechless wonder they fell back, staring at the animal.

" Ah ! " cried Macphie, " the black dog's day is drawing near."

In safety they crossed the sound and landed on Jura. Making immediately for the cave, they there made preparations for the night, collecting heather for their beds, and fuel for the fire. The day was then so far advanced that they determined to await the morrow before seeking the deer. They feasted on the provisions they had brought and seeking their couches early, passed the night without incident.

Next morning they arose at break of day and prepared for the chase ; but to their disgust the hound, which had seemed so eager to accompany them, now skulked again, crouching and refusing to leave the cave. Again the young men urged Macphie to destroy the creature ; but again he refused.

All that day the hunters spent on the hills and many were the stags that fell to their aim. Never had better sport rewarded their efforts. Weary and hungry they at length returned to the cave there to feast and to rest from their labours. A great fire was lighted, and around it they sat, while the smoke circled overhead, escaping at length from the aperture in the roof. The flames burned brightly, leaping, sparkling, and casting huge distorted shadows of the men upon the rocky walls around. Savoury were the venison steaks which they grilled upon the embers and from their horn cups they drank the usquebaugh while all was merriment and good cheer, as with song and tale they passed the hours away, late into the night. And none heeded the despised hound as he lay in a far corner of the cave, his muzzle on his paws, his eyes fixed ever on his master.

"We want but the one thing to complete our happiness," said one of the young men. " I would like well if my sweetheart could be with me at this time."

"And indeed I wish the same," cried another, until all the sixteen foster-brothers had expressed the same amorous longing.

Macphie at the moment was standing with his back to the fire, warming his legs, and he looked down at his sixteen foster-brothers as they lay around him. There was not one amongst them but was as fine a lad as any maid might choose as her lover.

" For my part," said he, " I am very content that my wife should be in her own home this night. It is enough for me to be here myself."

But still the young men daffed, laughing together and jesting in manner not always seemly, while in silence Macphie stood regarding them. After a time it seemed to him, that, though the fire still burned, the darkness around them had deepened, and that strange oppression hung in the air. Perhaps the young men too were sensible of this heaviness, for one after another fell silent, until complete stillness reigned within the cave. Even the fire ceased to crackle and the flames flickered and sank, leaving only the lurid light of dying embers.

Presently one of the young men violently arose, as if shaking himself free. He tried to laugh but his mirth sounded hollow. " I

think," said he, "that it is time we all went
to bed."

So one after the other arose and with few
added words they all retired, each to the spot
where he had prepared his sleeping place,
leaving Macphie standing by the fire alone,
and yet not quite alone, for at that moment,
stealthily, out of the darkened recess where it
had crouched unobserved, the black hound
crept and lay down at its master's feet.

How long Macphie stood there he could not
tell. Within the cave all was silence; but
presently from without issued the sound of
music, sweeter than ever he had heard, though
whether from human voices singing in
harmony, or from softly touched and throbbing
strings he knew not. It came and went like
the whisper of the evening wind. Then as he
listened amazed, he saw sixteen young and
lovely maidens entering, all dressed in green,
their tresses loose and floating around them.
Hand in hand they came, tripping, gliding,
noiselessly, beautiful as the moonlight on the
sea. But the black dog arose at their
approach, growling fiercely, the hair on its
back bristling, and the maidens held aloof.
Then unclasping their hands they stole to
where the sleeping men lay and were lost to
view. The music died away; silence fell again.
A deeper gloom seemed to gather within the

cave, unrelieved saving for a narrow circle of light from the embers of the fire.

Hours passed, perhaps only minutes—Macphie had lost count of time, standing there, as if spellbound. But at length he was aware of movements in the darkness and one after the other he saw the green clad maidens emerge from the shadows, noiselessly as if themselves shadows of the night, circling around him, their faces turned towards him. Seizing his dirk he hastily traced with its point a circle around himself and the hound on the ground. "The cross of Christ be upon me," he cried aloud. The echoes of his voice rang from the rocky walls and died away.

Slowly, slowly the wheeling forms receded, their faces still regarding him, but now no more alluring, smiling; but with anger and malevolence in their looks. Slowly, slowly they seemed to melt and vanish into the night.

Macphie looked down—the black hound crouched trembling at his feet. He looked around, "Alister! Hamish! Alan!" he called the names of his foster-brothers, but no answer came. What had befallen them, there in the darkness? He shouted again—only the echoes mocked him. Silence. Then, forgetful of his own peril in his fear for his companions, he leaped from the circle and would have rushed to their succour; but a hoarse cry broke from his lips and he staggered back; for a horror yet more fearful at once confronted him ; through the aperture of the cave's roof a monstrous hand and arm were reached, groping blindly for him. He felt his limbs failing him : benumbed, paralyzed he strove in vain to escape the clutch which sought to strangle him.   One hope only remained. " Black hound ! " he cried " save me now or I am undone."

And then ensued such a fight as never before had human eyes beheld, for, instantly, irresistible as the boulder launched from a hill-crest, the hound sprang, and seizing in its fangs the arm above the elbow, held fast. Hither and thither the great brute was flung, while its snarls and growls like thunder filled the cave.   In vain the arm strove to drag it upwards ; but with all its paws braced against the roof, the hound resisted. Like a flail the hand lashed to and fro.   It plucked, it tore, writhing, striving to rend and crush its adversary ; but the hound with indomitable courage fought it still.   And all the while Macphie stood watching, knowing that his life, and, for all he knew, his eternal welfare depended on the issue of that battle, and yet unable to move hand or foot.   Suddenly, by what magic he could not tell, it seemed to him as if the hand, unable by strength to gain the victory, had beckoned the very fires of Hell to its aid, for all around the hound he saw what seemed like lambent flames and spirals of blue smoke which flickered and wreathed. And yet undaunted the faithful defender maintained its hold. Then, in a moment, came the victory ; the arm, severed from the shoulder, dropped upon the ground. But even then its horror continued ; for still, like a crushed snake, it moved convulsively, quivered for a few moments, stretched herself at length and lay apparently lifeless.

The hound, too, had fallen gasping at Macphie's feet, exhausted, perhaps dying. But one last effort remained to be accomplished by it; for next instant the massive rocks round about them shook to what seemed to be the trampling of a huge body overhead and a dreadful shrieking rent the air. Immediately the hound sprang once more to its feet, and bounding from the cave, rushed to attack the thing which threatened from above. But what it encountered out there, in the night, and what occurred in that encounter none can say, for no human eye beheld. Only the thunderous trampling ceased and the awful screams were hushed.

Stock still and rigid stood Macphie, there in the cave alone, waiting, listening, still unable to move hand or foot. Beside him lay

the lifeless arm. No movement, no sound
came from the shadows in which lay his foster
brothers. He dared not speak, hardly dared
to breathe. Only the dying embers of the fire
shed a faint illumination around him ; but
even these at length faded, leaving him in
complete darkness, silence, saving for the
distant muttering of the restless sea. Hour
after hour passed by. Perhaps standing there
he slept ; perhaps spellbound as he was, all
thought was banished from his mind ; for
quite suddenly he became aware of the dawn
of another day. A rosy light suffused the
cave. The breath of morning stirred the
heavy stagnant air and then, as if bands had
been cast from him, movement was restored.
Sinking on his knees he crossed himself and
sprang upright. Dimly he could see the
forms of his foster-brothers where they lay ;
but none stirred. He called again their
names ; but none answered. A terrible fear
smote him and he rushed to arouse one who
lay nearest to him. He flung himself on his
knees by the recumbent man, tore the plaid
from his face—a face of deathly pallor.
He shook him, but recoiled from the contact,
for the form which he shook was stiff and cold
—dead. With a cry Macphie arose and flung
himself from one to another of the men. The
same fate had overtaken all. All lay dead.

Staggering blindly Macphie fled from that cave of horror and death, out to where the first streaks of dawn reddened the East and the sea, blood red, stretched before him. Escape home, somehow he must—leave behind him forever the terrors of that night. His boat! his boat! But hardly had he proceeded ten yards in his mad flight when something tripped him and he fell headlong. Rolling over he found that he had stumbled on the body of his hound. That faithful defender, too, lay dead ; but he at least should not be left behind. Kneeling, Macphie strained to lift the great carcase. And then befell that which of all his experiences of the night was the most appalling, like to have unbalanced his already overburdened mind and sent him as a madman, screaming to oblivion in the sea. Somewhere from the heavy mist which still clung shroudlike around the hills, a shrill unearthly whistle pierced the air, again and yet again. As if the very blood within his veins were frozen, as if his heart had been arrested by that ghostly call, Macphie remained motionless, listening. He dared not look ; but suddenly from the cave behind him a strange sound reached his ears—the sound of stealthy crawling, such as a great snake might make, writhing slowly, furtively across the pebbles and granite of the ground. What

it was Macphie knew not, only that it was not
human.   As he listened he heard it pause,
as if regarding him.   Again, as if impatient
of delay, the whistle shrilled and with a yell
Macphie leapt to his feet and turned.   Something flashed past him from the cave's mouth,
like a snake propelling itself convulsively,
over the pebbles, betwixt the rocks, up the
hillside into the mist in answer to the summons,
to be seen by the islanders no more.

Though he should perish in his intrusion,
Macphie felt that he must re-enter the cave
and see whether all was as it had been.   A
courage as of madness possessed him.   Shouting defiance he rushed within.   One glance
sufficed to show him that the severed arm lay
there no longer.   In an instant he was out
again, dragged the body of the hound and
pitched it into the waiting boat.   With the
strength of a madman he launched the craft
and madly plied the oars.

From the quay at Colonsay they watched
in wonder the approach of that solitary boatman.   They crowded around him, assisting
him ashore.   They questioned him eagerly,
staring in dismay at his ghastly face, and at
the terror in his eyes. But not for many a day
would he answer their questioning.   They
would have lifted the body of the hound and
pitched it in the sea ; but with sudden ferocity

he flung them back, pointing at the body. They grouped, gazing in wonder at it, for its bones were crushed as by a giant hand and its coat was scorched as if flames had licked around it.

C

THYRA.

Thig crioch air an saoghal,
Ach mairidh gaol is ceòl.

The world will pass away,
But love and music last for aye.

LOCH Maree! The very name is lovely,
and lovely too, that long lake, as it lies
beneath the shadows of the slumbering
hills. In winter you shall see it in grandeur,
lashed by tempestuous winds which, gathering
their battalions in the glens, rush shrieking
forth at length to drive the snow or hail, like
sheeted ghosts, over the tormented waves;
for never (so men say) are these waters frozen.
You shall see the deep snow-wreaths heaped,
smothering the world around and silencing
all sounds of life; or, when an angry sun looks
sullenly from dark clouds, the frosted fretwork
of the ice upon the shore will sparkle as if
innumerable gems had been scattered there.
Here autumn holds royal court, and spring
her revels for her tender children; but in the
long hush of the summer evening is the loch
seen best of all; when so stilled are the waters
that they mirror in flawless perfection the

beautiful face of Nature bent above ; when
every cloud and hill and every leaf of the
slender birch trees overshadowing are pictured
perfectly, saving only where the lazily-feeding
trout disturb with expanding rings the crystal
surface. No sound breaks the silence ; the
last melancholy piping of the curlew has
passed ; the chuckle of the grouse roosting
in the heather has ceased. The long vista
of the purple hills seems to melt, blending
with the shadows of the coming night.
Yonder is a wooded isle; above it a bright star
already twinkles in the clear amethyst of the
sky. In the far valleys night is brooding;
peace unfolds her wings; sleep descends, sleep
with her dreams of long ago. Years, centuries,
roll aside ; shades of the past steal into the
twilight. . . . .

     *   *   *   *   *

She was most beautiful. Like the dawn her
face—a pallor from which shone the starlight
of her eyes, over-shadowed by the dark
mystery of her hair. A princess, too, daughter
of the royal house of Ulster. Many had sought
to wed her ; but none could win her, for she
was not as other maidens of her father's court
—laughter-loving and gay. She shrank from
the boisterous revels of the castle hall, the
feasting and the minstrelsy, loving better to
wander solitary by quiet streams or in wood-

lands, where, sitting on the moss beneath the shade of the great overarching boughs, she would sing softly, with none to hear.   Tender-hearted, too, she was, to all weak and suffering creatures : even a little bird with broken wing she would care for and cherish until its hurt was healed.   Her brothers mocked her and in vain would urge her to join with them in the chase ; but their mockery ceased before the serene tranquility of her gaze, so that, abashed and silenced, they turned away.

At length the king, her father, wearying of the complaints of her rejected suitors and unable himself to understand her tempera-ment, determined that a cloister should receive her, and with his suggestion she gladly con-curred.   A kinswoman of the royal family was at that time the gentle and pious superior of the Convent of Inch Cailleach on the distant Scottish Loch Lomond.   And thither the king planned to send his daughter with her atten-dant maids, an escort being promised by the Lord of the Isles.   All had gone well with the band of travellers until the shores of Loch Maree had been reached, and the little isle, where dwelt a few aged monks, was in sight, when disaster befell :   a lawless bandit, known as Red Hector of the Hills, and his robber band had fallen on the clansmen of MacDonald* and slain

* MacDonald was Lord of the Isles.

them. The princess had been seized by the
outlaw himself and would have been carried
to his mountain cave, but for the sudden
intervention of the monks whom not even
Red Hector would defy—so great was the
veneration in which they were held. The
princess with her maidens were hurried in a
boat to the island and there found refuge,
dwelling in a little guest house apart, there
awaiting an opportunity to escape. A
messenger was found to carry the news of her
misfortune to the King of Ulster, asking for
rescue ; but week after week had passed
and no succour had reached them. They
dared not venture from this sanctuary, for
Red Hector had vowed to recapture her, and
they knew that he and his men kept vigilant
watch upon the isle. Often the princess would
sit alone by her window, gazing out on the
still loch as sunset flamed over the western
hills and purple shadows deepened in the glens.
And sometimes she would fancy, as if in a
vision, that from the dim golden glory, in
which sky and loch seemed to merge, a white-
sailed ship came sailing, silently as a dream.
She seemed to hear sweet, faint notes as of a
silver bugle call. And as the boat drew near
she saw, standing on the prow, a youth more
noble in bearing than any she had ever beheld,
and he smiled and beckoned her to come, to

sail with him from captivity, away to the lovely
land of sunset and of dreams. But always,
as if weighted by leaden fetters, she seemed
unable to move hand or foot, and sadly the
youth had sailed away, fading from her view.

Not even to her maidens did Thyra tell her
secret : it was hidden within her heart ; but
always when sunset was golden she would
steal alone to her window and wait and watch,
longing for her waking dream, sad at heart
when, as sometimes befell, she waited in vain.

At times one of the holy fathers would row
to the mainland in the hope of hearing tidings
of another escort sent to guard the princess
and her maidens on their southern way ; but
always his efforts had been unrewarded. Still
rumour told of the presence of Red Hector
lurking near. At length one of the monks
determined to extend his enquiries further
than hitherto had been done, and for this
purpose he would absent himself for a whole
night, returning at sundown of the following
day. He was rowed across the channel accordingly by a companion by whom the boat was
brought back, the place and hour for his
return having been appointed.

All the day of the old monk's absence Thyra
waited, confident somehow that succour was
near, eager for escape, and yet with a vague
and wayward sense of regret that she should

leave that sweet isle—the island of her dreams.
Restlessly she wandered to and fro, counting
the hours, or sat gazing at the sunlit waters
and beyond these to the billowing hills and
rugged crags, all silent, steeped in sleep.

It seemed impossible that a scene so fair and
peaceful could harbour the violence and
passions of evil men.

Hour after hour passed. Evening came at
length and sunset; but with them no waking
dream—she was too intent on her vigil,
longing for the return of the old monk. She
thrilled with strange and conflicting emotions,
expectancy of what she knew not. One of
the fathers was to row to the mainland before
nightfall to meet the other returning from his
quest. She determined to forestall the plan;
she herself would cross the loch. The little
monastery bell was tinkling to announce the
vesper hour. Her maidens were occupied.
Unobserved, she reached the beach, cast off
the boat from its moorings, and pushed out.
A wild-duck squattered from her approach;
but no other sign of life disturbed the scene.
She rowed swiftly, so that ere many minutes
had passed, the boat glided beneath the overhanging leaves of clustering birch trees, and she
stepped on shore. Here was the appointed
meeting place; but though she peeped
cautiously from the shelter of the leaves she

could see no one. She listened. Only an
oozel, perched upon a stone, piped its little lay.
Silence. Still sheltered by the leaves she sat
there waiting, thinking perhaps of the
cloistered life which lay before her, a life in
which perpetual peace would surely be found,
remote from the world. Suddenly she was
aroused from her reverie. Far distant she
saw the old monk toiling along a path by the
loch side, staff in hand.

In a moment she was on her feet, had broken
through the boughs and was running to meet
him.

"You, my daughter," cried the old man.
" And have you come alone ? "

"Yes, Father," she smiled. "My maidens
are milking the goats and the holy brethren
pray ; so I have come alone."

"That is rash, my daughter, for you knew
not what my tidings may be."

"What of him ? "

"All is well. The Holy Virgin guards you.
He has gone, though only for a time, on some
sinful foray."

"We may escape ? "

"Not yet. To-morrow or the next day
he may return; nothing is certain. We must
await until all is sure. He is wicked and
cunning ; though, the Saints be praised, not
so wicked that he dare violate our sanctuary."

" And my father ? "

" Alas, no word yet has come from your royal father. But succour he will surely send, for many of the great chiefs are his friends and they will quickly revenge the violence of this rude outlaw who threatens you, and you will yet be conveyed safely to the reverend Mother and Sisters who await you."

" I pray that it may be so."

" Come, my daughter."

Together they retraced the path towards the boat and were about to enter it on their return to the isle, when from the hillside at hand a sound arrested them—the note of a bugle call, silvery, faint and far. In consternation the old man turned towards the princess, but he saw no fear in her eyes, only a look of glad expectancy.

" Quick," he bade. " Hide beneath the leaves."

She suffered herself to be drawn beneath shelter, but her lips smiled and her eyes still sought the hills. So they waited, motionless, silent. Then they heard him as he crashed through the brushwood on the slopes, heard his footsteps pause, close at hand, and again his bugle call and a shout. It was his hound that he summoned, for they heard him chiding it for its wandering, and turn as if to depart.

He never guessed their presence hidden but a
few feet from him, crouching there.   But the
hound betrayed them, suddenly thrusting
itself through the thick branches, glaring at
the refugees, its bristles rising.   It barked
furiously.

"What now? What now?" asked its
master, and, parting the boughs, he started
back at sight of the old man and the maid
and for a moment laid his hand on his sword-
hilt.   "Who are you?" he cried.

Discovered they arose and stepped forth
from their concealment, regarding anxiously
the stranger before them.   Tall, blue-eyed,
fair, dressed as no native of the land would be
clad, they knew that he must have come from
some far country.   And though his voice was
pleasant his speech was halting—that of no
Gael.

"I am, as you see, an old man," the monk
replied.   He took Thyra's hand, "and this,"
he added, "is a maiden under my protection."

The young man gazed in silence at the
princess and seemed unable to remove his look
from her loveliness.   Her eyes, too, met his
and lingered for a moment ; until, like the
flush of dawn, a rosy glow slowly suffused the
pallor of her face.   Ashamed, she bowed her
head.

"And you who question us," the monk

interrupted their thoughts ; " who are you ? "
"That matters not."

"Suffer us then to go upon our way,"
pleaded the old man, and drawing Thyra's
arm beneath his own he would have turned
back.

But the stranger, in a stride, advanced, and,
laying his hand upon the shoulder of the other,
detained him. "Not yet," he forbade.

Half in fear for his ward the monk angrily
attempted to shake off the arresting hand.
"By what right do you thus rudely hinder
us ? " he demanded.

"Before I let you go you must tell me this
maiden's name."

Trembling in impotent wrath, the monk
refused : "To no churlish wayfarer such as
you shall I tell her name."

The young man's face crimsoned. "Had
one less reverend in appearance than you
dared to call me churl," he retorted, "I
should have laid his head as low as his heels.
Know that I am a prince, son of the King of
Denmark. I have come as the guest of
MacKenzie to hunt the deer, and here I have
lost my companions and my way."

Upon this the old monk's wrath was
instantly cooled. He humbly craved pardon
and told the prince both Thyra's name and

parentage, and the cause of her taking sanctuary on the island.

With burning indignation the prince listened to his story, and when it was ended he turned towards Thyra. "Lady," he said, "I know not yet how best I can serve you, but a way shall be found. One fate only I fear—lest having once beheld you, I should see your face no more."

She looked up, smiling. "You little guess, Sir," she said, "how often ere this I have seen you, and I shall surely see you again in . . in that sweet land where we have met."

" I do not understand," he cried, and would have seized her hand.

But she eluded him, and leaping lightly into the boat, assisted the monk to embark. As they pushed out from the shore she turned to wave adieu to the prince, and smiled again to see him still standing, perplexity in his gaze.

*   *   *   *   *   *

We follow now the fortunes of the prince. He at length found his way home, but there discovered all in confusion. MacKenzie and his retainers had had to depart in haste to guard a distant part of their territory upon which an enemy had made an incursion. The prince and his men had been left to the care of those unfit for battle who remained in the castle. Thus all immediate prospect of enlist-

ing the sympathies of the chief on behalf of
the wronged damsel was lost. All night the
young Dane lay wakeful, recalling every look,
every word which had been exchanged in his
interview with Thyra ; or slept, only to see
her beautiful face smile again in his dreams.
Before break of day he hastened to the loch
side where he had met her. He could see the
wooded isle of her sanctuary, vague as a vision
through the morning mist. He heard the
sweet, distant music of the monastery bell
wafted over the waters ; but no sign of life,
no movement. He stretched forth his arms.
" Thyra," he cried, " maid of the morning in
whose eyes shine the tender light of dawn,
awake and come to me." He listened.—
Silence.

" Darkly the night lingers in the glens ; but
darker the shadow on my heart when you are
absent. The little birds awake and call you.
The whispering wind of morning breathes your
name. The whole world is desolate without
you, but more desolate my soul. Thyra,
awake and come to me."

Only the echoes mocked him. The eastern
horizon flamed crimson and flushed the mist
which hung on the hills, and lay, like a fleecy
coverlet, on the sleeping waters of the loch.
The mountain tops caught the glory of the
sunrise and glowed like beacon lights. In the

western heaven the stars paled and faded ;
while from a glen near by a stag bellowed his
welcome to the coming day, and, hidden in the
heather, a grouse shook the dewdrops from his
wings and chuckled joyously as morning broke.
But still the prince waited in vain. Only
when night again fell did he, despairingly,
turn homeward.

All next day he watched again, and again
in vain. Two days, three days passed thus,
and still his patient vigil was unrewarded.
Unable longer to endure this delay he resolved
himself to cross the loch to the island and there
to seek out the lady without whom he felt
that life no longer could be endured. After
wandering far, he at last found a man who
owned a boat, and him he persuaded to row
him to his destination.

Again the morning sun shone as they made
preparation for the crossing. The owner of the
boat was a wretched creature, unkempt and savage, with restless eyes, overhung by his matted
hair, which looked furtively at the prince.
His abode was a cabin, rude and half ruinous.
From its mud-plastered stones and neglected
thatch the long grass waved. The prince
mistrusted him, but from no other could a boat
be had, so the craft was launched ; but leaving it with its stern still resting on the shore,
the Highlander stood for a moment, and,

putting his fingers to his lips, blew a long,
shrill whistle. In a moment the prince's
dagger was at his throat; but the man
cowered with signs and half articulate
mutterings, protesting his innocence and,
seizing the oars, urged the boat from the land.
Seated as he was the prince did not see the
hill side left behind, nor the scowling faces
which peered from the heather, watching his
departure.

He reached at length the humble abode of
the monks and knocked loudly at the door of
what seemed to be the principal dwelling.
One who was unknown to him answered his
summons, and to him the prince told the purpose of his visit; but the monk sternly bade
him dismiss from his mind all thought of her
who was about to enter the religious life.
The prince, however, was not thus to be turned
away and demanded to see the Head of the
little community. After some delay the aged
monk whom he had previously met, came to
the door and to him once more the prince
made his request that he might be permitted
an interview with the princess Thyra.

"My son," said the old ecclesiastic, "she
whom you seek is about to become the bride
of Christ. To no words from an earthly lover,
therefore, should she lend her ears."

"From her own lips only, shall I take her

denial of my suit, however," the prince
vehemently declared.

A little group of the old men had meanwhile
gathered behind their superior, anxiously
peering past him at the bold intruder. Towards them the abbot—if such he were—now
turned, and they whispered hurriedly in conference. What the outcome of this delibera-
tion might have been it is impossible to say ;
for before any conclusion had been reached
they were suddenly interrupted by the
approach of Thyra herself. She with her
maidens had stepped from the little dwelling allotted to them, and stood behind the
prince.

He heard their light footsteps and turned.
" Princess," he cried and, kneeling, kissed her
hand.

A tender light shone in her eyes as she bade
him arise.

" Princess," he cried again, " if I indeed
intrude upon a seclusion here which you would
fain maintain, as these holy men declare,
then bid me go, and though my heart be so
heavy that I must sink beneath these waters,
yet will I obey. But if you will grant me
speech with you alone, if even for a few
moments, then will my heart soar, and sing,
I think, for evermore."

" I will speak with you, Sir," she whispered.

So he led her by the hand, the fathers
frowning ; but the maidens smiling to see them
go. He followed a path all overgrown with
heavy boughs, and these he parted that she
might pass through towards the western shore
of the island. Very silent were they, for a
time ; but presently as the joyful sunlight
dappled their way and happy birds sang overhead, and bright flowers broke as if rioting
in joy about their feet, their hearts were so
uplifted in sheer delight of a lovely world,
that, like children free from care, they laughed
and ran together, still hand in hand.

Out of breath, they sank at length upon a
mossy bank, the cool fronds of the bracken
laying light touch upon them, the ripples of
the loch running in to welcome them as with
laughter, while before them lay the vista of
the hills and loch—a vision glorious in the
splendour of the summer sun.

Lying there at her feet he listened while
she told him of the rude rioting of her father's
court, and of the clamour, violence, and warfare in which her tribesmen delighted, of how
she had longed for peace. And in turn he
spoke of the distant land over which, should
he live, he was destined one day to reign.
Then after a time grown restless, still as might
children, they fashioned for themselves a
bower, interlacing tender boughs of birch tree

D

and trailing ivies. They carpeted it with moss and hung it about with hair-bells ; and beneath its shade they sat again. He had hung at his girdle a bag containing simple food ; and they had found a wild honey comb; so on these, and clear water from the loch, they feasted and were content. Thus they beguiled the long day until the sun had set and twilight fell upon the quiet world, and one pale star shone above them in the blue. Whether the good fathers sought and failed to find them, hidden in their bower as they were ; or whether these men of peace feared to anger the prince by intruding on his wooing —in either case the lovers were left undisturbed.

No word of love had passed their lips ; and at length silence fell between them, as side by side they looked out at the dim purple of the hills and the deepening shadows of the coming night.

After a time, still gazing before him, " All my life," he said, " it seems to me that I have sought you, and now, having found you, I know well that I could never live but with you near."

Her head drooped, but she did not answer.

" It may be," he continued, " that I have no right to tell you that I love you, you who have thought to cast off all earthly ties ; yet God who made you decreed that you should be the one woman in all this world for me. Look at that star." He pointed. "It is the star of my love. Will you let it lead you, for it will shine forever ? "

Still she returned no word.

He bowed his face upon his hands. "You do not love me," he moaned. "I shall never see your face again."

A moment's silence ; a touch as of a rose-leaf fell upon his hair. He looked up. Her face was bent above him. Her lips smiled. Her eyes looked steadfastly in his own. He gazed at first incredulously ; then, reading there a wonderful message, with a great cry : "Thyra ! Thyra ! " he reached his arms towards her as she sank upon his breast.

"I have dreamed of you," she whispered. "In visions you have come to me, when all the universe was hushed, but for the beating of my heart." And with her head pillowed on his shoulders she told him her waking dreams of a white-sailed ship which sailed from the twilight-mingling of water and of sky, bearing him on its prow ; but ever passing away again.

"It was my restless soul that sought the sweet haven of your heart," he answered. "And so you knew me when we met ? "

She looked up, smiling, " I should know that you were near though I lay within the grave."

Perhaps it was the thought of that cold and final resting-place; perhaps it was but a chill breath which blew from the descending night which caused her to shiver in his arms.

Instantly he was all anxiety for her. " You are cold," he cried. " I have kept you here too long after sundown. I must lead you back." And gently he raised her to her feet.

But she clung to him, trembling. " I have a fear," she said, " a dreadful fear."

" Of what ? " he laughed.

" It is of Red Hector of the hills," she whispered. " Promise me that you will avoid him ? "

" My life and all that I have, saving only my honour, I would lay at your feet," he evaded, kissing her lips.

Slowly they retraced their way until the monastery was within sight. There he left her standing, looking after him as he ran down the steep path to the shore. Once he turned to wave farewell and saw her still motionless ; then the intervening trees hid her from his view.

He had forgotten all about the boatman ; but he found that uncouth pilot still patiently awaiting him. He therefore bade the man row to the mainland. So full of joy was the

prince's heart that he paid no heed to the
scowling looks of the other. He would have
conversed with him ; but being answered in
monosyllables or in unintelligible mutterings,
laughingly desisted and fell to singing.
Arrived at the landing place he paid and dismissed the man, and set out on his long tramp
homeward. The lovely face of his lady was
still in his thoughts as he trudged along.
Hardly it seemed possible that such good fortune had befallen him as to win her love ;
impossible to believe that the world around
him was the same as that through which he
had passed but a few hours before. He
laughed aloud in the sheer joy of life. At
length he reached a turning on his way—a
shoulder of the hill, by a deep ravine through
which a noisy burn tumbled, after passing
which the still dimly seen island would be
lost to view. He paused, therefore, to take
one last look. He thought of her there—his
bride, his queen to be. "Sweet love," he
cried, "goodnight."

Something whizzed past—a thud upon the
bank beside him. What was that ? He
stooped and plucked an arrow from the ground.
He peered into the shadows of the glen. In an
instant, his cap, transfixed by another missile,
was dashed from his head. He sprang backwards, his drawn sword in his hand. Twenty

yards ahead of him a giant boulder stood, and from behind its shelter suddenly stepped a man—a Highlander in native attire, his chest half exposed, his arms and knees bare and shaggy with hair which matched the red tangle of his locks and beard. From beneath his frowning brows his eyes flashed, either with madness or fury. Casting aside his bow he drew his claymore and stood stock still—a wild and ferocious figure.

For a moment the prince stared speechlessly at this formidable opponent ; but not yet had he lost his sense of goodwill to a world in which he himself had found such happiness ; so it was with more of jest than resentment that he asked : "Who, and what are you who bar my way, and would make a target of my body ? "

Slowly, with eyes which never wavered in their fixed intensity of gaze, the Highlander advanced until some six paces only separated the men. " Do you not know me ? " he asked in deep, guttural tones which reverberated with passion. "Have you never heard of Red Hector of the hills ? If not, you see him now and shall feel his skill."

At the mention of that name the prince stiffened and a new and dangerous gleam shone in his eyes. " I have indeed heard of you, Red Hector," he answered, " as one who makes war on defenceless women and old men."

The Highlander's bosom heaved and he blew from distended nostrils like an angry bull. "You lie," he bellowed, "in fair fight I slew the men of her escort, and left unscathed both her and the holy fathers."

"If you speak, as I suppose, of the princess Thyra, is she not in sanctuary in yonder island, seeking refuge from your cowardly and brutal violence?"

"And if she be, it is a sanctuary which I, at least, have respected, while you, accursed hound, have sought to sneak thither in secret. You supposed that you could elude Red Hector, and pass unseen; but you could no more escape my vigilance than you can escape me now, and here and now we shall settle the score between us."

"Very gladly," the prince smiled: "so that you fight fair."

"Fight fair!" Red Hector repeated furiously. "Do you suppose I could not have shot you dead but a moment past, had I so willed? Could I not have bidden my men await with me here, so that, surrounded, you must in a moment have been hacked to pieces? You have but a hunting knife to match my dirk. See! I throw that weapon and target, too, away." He flung his dirk and shield from him as he spoke. "Sword against sword only, I will fight you to the death."

In an instant steel clashed on steel as the swordsmen fell into position. The Highlander was the more heavily armed and by far the stronger man ; but the Dane was nimble and, unlike his opponent, relied less on the cut than on the lightning thrust of his weapon. Backwards, forwards the fight swayed, as first one and then the other pressed to the attack.

It seemed hardly possible that human eye and hand could foresee and foil the fury that flashed and played like baleful wildfire in the air. With grim, set faces and eyes which never for an instant left the eyes of the other, in silence, but for the ring of metal on metal, their panting breath and the thud of their footsteps on the ground, they fought for their lives.

The Highlander had thought to find an easy victim, but now as his efforts proved unavailing, his rage redoubled.

By sheer brute force he sought to sweep aside the slender blade which seemed ever to quiver at his breast, and more than once he bounded clear of its point only by a hair's breadth. Goaded, at length, to madness, he seemed to throw discretion to the winds ; for with a yell he suddenly rushed in upon his adversary, as if to grapple with him hand to hand. But, light of foot as a deer, the prince sprang back, avoiding the charge, and, ere the other could regain the defensive, he thrust with all his might. Even then, so quick was Red Hector, that by a half turn he almost escaped the point ; but not quite ; for the weapon wounded his breast, and the impact of the hilt sent him staggering nearly to the ground.

Then and there the prince might have ended the affair ; but he leaped back and with lowered sword regarded his adversary. "You have fought well," he praised, " and honour demands no more. Promise to leave the lady yonder unmolested and we may part as friends."

Like a wounded beast Red Hector glared at him, his lips drawn back, his bared teeth gleaming from beneath his beard. " You are afraid." he taunted. " You count a scratch such as you have given me your victory, and think to escape my vengeance. Fool and coward, you little know Red Hector of the hills ! "

The prince laughed, and for an instant, turned his face contemptuously aside. But that instant had nearly proved fatal ; for, quick as an adder strikes, Red Hector sprang, his broadsword whistled through the air and smote the young man's side. The blow was of such terrific violence that it might almost have cloven him in two, had his belt and hunting knife not intervened to break its force ; but it sent him reeling to the ground. His head struck a stone, he quivered and lay senseless, the blood pouring from his wound.

Red Hector bent above the fallen man who lay, to all appearance, dead. He kicked the prostrate form as he might the carcase of a dog ; then, gathering up his dirk and target, and without another look at his victim, he strode away.

But the prince was not dead. He had been stunned by the crash of his head against the stone, and after a few moments the agony of his wounded side recalled him to his senses. He looked up. Twilight was fading ; night descended, and in the clear heavens the stars twinkled impassively above him. He listened—only the burn in the ravine splashed and murmured its heedless song. He strove to arise : but with a groan he sank back again ; for movement was intolerable, and the blood spurted from his side. Were that stream to flow unchecked he knew that he must die ; so, painfully, he shifted his belt and tightened it above the wound so that the bleeding was staunched. Hour after hour passed by and darkness lay on the land. Whispering voices seemed to awake from the bracken and the heather.   He thought of his own dear country and the home which he might never see again. And then the face of his love seemed to look on him with tender pity in her eyes. For her sweet sake he must not die, must not leave her still in peril. With a great cry: "Thyra! Thyra! Come to me," he broke the silence; but only the echoes answered him: "Thyra, Thyra."

Thirst. Thirst. His lips were parched. He must drink or perish, and yet, the agony when he stirred! That renewed stream from his side! Yet better to bleed to death than die of thirst. Desperately, pressing his hand above his wound, inch by inch he dragged himself, groaning, towards the burn, reached it at length, drank, and then the stars seemed to wheel a fiery trail above him. He heard as it were the roar of many waters. Darkness closed over him.

*　*　*　*　*　*

Sweet dreams soothing a tired mind. Somewhere a happy bird singing. Fragrance as of flowers in sunshine. Ah! but so languid, so weak! Enough to lie with closed eyes that his dreams might be unbroken. Was he dead? And this a new world of quietness on which he had entered? He could not tell, could not think, But if he had passed to a spirit land, it had been through great suffering. Yes, there had been troubled dreams, too, dreams of a furnace of pain, an agony unendurable in which he had cried aloud for death to end his anguish. But a cool hand laid upon his brow had brought relief, and tender arms laid around him had hushed the turmoil of his torments. Now all distress was ended, and only a vision remained of a sweet face bent above him, of eyes wet with tears of pity and of love, the face of his beloved, of Thyra. Some danger had threatened her, some peril from which he alone could save her ; but what ? —He could not remember. Perhaps even now she had need of his protection. He must go to her, find her. He opened his eyes, struggling feebly to raise himself—was he dreaming still ? That dear face, so pale, so anxious, instantly leaning over him ! It could be but a dream, a dream which he longed might last for ever. He gazed in wonder. " Thyra," he whispered.

Tenderly, tenderly she caught him to her, laid his head on her bosom, kneeling by his side, her lips pressed on his brow. " My beloved, my beloved ! "

She was no vision ; but his own dear lady, princess of his heart. " Tell me, tell me . . .," he entreated.

" Hush, hush, dear heart ! " she bade. " Lie still, lie still." As if he had been a little child she rocked him.

And like a child he was content to rest his head upon her breast and await until she should make known to him where he was, and all that had befallen to bring him there. Smiling, in listless contentment, he fell asleep.

When he again awaked he looked about him, eagerly seeking her ; but she was nowhere to be seen. Instead he saw the familiar forms of his own faithful followers standing by his bed, and beside them the old monk whom he had at first encountered. " Where is she ? Where is the princess ? " he asked eagerly.

The father approached him. " She will return, my son," he promised ; " but she, too, sorely needs rest."

The prince looked about him and saw a small, barely-furnished room. On the wall above his bed hung a rudely-carved Crucifix, and through the open window he looked on the green branches of trees, and beyond them, lay a sunlit view of the loch and distant hills. " Where am I ? And how came I here ? " he asked.

" You have been very near to death," the old monk told him ; " but, the Saints be praised, you will recover now ; meanwhile, you are safe within our island sanctuary."

" How long have I been here ? "

" For many weeks, my son."

The island ! For many weeks ! And then

slowly the memory of that evening, now long passed, returned, when he had met Red Hector of the hills—his wound, and that agonising crawl that he might drink. " But how came I here ? " he asked again.

" Listen then, my son, and I shall tell you. After your visit to the island, many weeks ago, the princess was full of fear for you, the more so when one told her that you had been conveyed in the boat of mad Ian—a man who owns as master Red Hector. Next morning therefore she prevailed on us to row to the mainland and there make enquiries concerning you. I myself, with one other, crossed, and found you wounded and uncon- scious. We carried you back with us and sent for your followers who, too, are here. From that time until now the princess and they have nursed you day and night."

" How can I thank you, Father ? " asked the prince. " As for her—if as my wife she will return with me, the life which she has restored to me shall be devoted to her service."

" That is as God wills, my son," answered the monk.

For many days the prince lay slowly recover- ing his strength. But, though the princess still tended him, her visits were less frequent and less prolonged as his health renewed. When however at length he could be borne by his men to lie without in the sunshine, then always she would sit by his side, and thus they passed many happy hours together as they watched the shadows of the clouds flit over the quiet hills and the changeful face of the waters. Nature herself seemed to smile on these happy lovers ; for day after day the sky was cloudless, and the summer breezes, laden with the scent of flowers, blew gently, as if toying with the stray ringlets of Thyra's hair. Indeed the young man and maid seemed themselves to be the children of the sunshine ; for in their beauty and joy it had been hard to find their like. Gradually, as time passed, the pallor left his cheeks ; and though her face had always been fair, it now seemed irradiated by an added loveliness. Even the stern monks, seeing them, would pause for a moment and smile indulgently—and perhaps a little sadly— ere passing on with downcast looks.

Sometimes he would tell her of his home across the sea, his father's court, and how all would love and honour her there, not merely as his bride, but for her own sweet sake. A ship would bear them to a life of peace and joy for ever.

And sometimes she would sing to him very softly, that none but he might hear ; and in her song she would tell him how she would follow him to the world's end, even were he no prince at all, but only a humble beggar with naught to offer her but the stars for their canopy and the woodland glades for their palace.

One day as they sat looking towards the mainland they saw a great concourse of men winding by the loch-side, but the distance between was so great that there could be no certainty whether these invaders had approached for warlike or for peaceful purposes. The princess at once fled to give the alarm to the monks, and presently the whole band of holy men had assembled to watch with the lovers those who approached. They saw a boat put out and presently it drew near. When it, at length, was but a stone's throw from shore, the princess with a glad cry ran to meet it, for she had recognised among the occupants an old man—one of her father's most trusted captains. Eagerly she asked if all were well and if he and his followers had come to escort her on her way to Loch Lomond.

But sorrowfully the old soldier told her that her father lay adying, and had sent this band to convey her home that he might bid her a last farewell.

Thyra wept bitterly at these tidings, nor could she be consoled though the prince himself tried to comfort her. Without delay she determined to set forth and bade her maidens prepare for their journey, retiring with them for that purpose. The Ulstermen, too, were taken within by the fathers for refreshment.

The prince left thus alone grieved sorely that his lady love should be taken from him, and a great foreboding of disaster overcast his mind. He was not yet sufficiently recovered of his wound to accompany her, and he dreaded to think of the perils which might befall her on her journey. But presently, as he sat moodily, he heard behind him the patter of lightly running feet and the flutter of garments and, ere he could turn his head, Thyra herself was kneeling by his side, her tearful eyes upraised, and her arms around him.

"Ah, my true love! How shall I leave you?" she cried.

For a time he could not answer; only he held her very closely to his breast. Then: "If I could but accompany you," said he.

"And so you shall," she vowed. "Day and night I shall hold you in my heart and the very thought of you shall be my guide and protector from all harm."

"The hours," said he, "which hold me here apart from you, will seem as lead."

"Nay," she corrected, "the hours shall be a golden chain to draw us together ever more."

E

" If ought of ill should befall you . . . ," he shuddered.

And " God keep you, O, my beloved," she breathed.

But presently she raised her face, looking past him, and her eyes, though turned towards the little chapel behind them, seemed as if wistfully gazing on a prophetic vision seen by her alone.   She smiled.

" What do you see ? " he asked.

" I see myself as your bride," she answered, and then, a faint blush tingeing the pallor of her cheeks, she hid her face on his breast again. "I saw ourselves, in a vision, united for ever. Oh, such a sweet vision ! "

He, too, turned towards the chapel.   " We shall be wedded there."

" Yes," she promised, " on my return we shall be wedded there, and then we shall sail away from strife and turmoil to a land of peace and joy, where we may live and love forever."

" On a white-sailed ship we shall sail away," he whispered.

Silence fell between them for a time, but suddenly she leaped to her feet ; for at that moment the fathers emerged from the monastery, leading with them the Ulstermen who were urgent to be gone.   And so all fell to bustle and much interchange of talk.   The princess herself had to hasten to her maidens to see whether their preparations for their journey were completed ; and meanwhile the boat was remanned, the crew resting on their outspread oars.

And so once more the prince was left alone ; but not for long, for soon she came again, this time with her maidens behind her, the men bearing the baggage to the boat. Only for a moment she paused, fighting down her tears, striving to whisper, " Farewell, beloved."

" God keep you," was all he could answer.

For a few moments he lay as if stunned. He could hear the men shouting from the boat, the splash of oars—repeated, fainter and ever fainter as distance widened. He must see her again, at all costs. He dragged himself to his feet, staggered and nearly fell, but steadied himself again. With out-stretched arms he reeled forward, feeble step by step, until he stood upon the bank in view of the loch. The boat was not yet so far but that he could see his love as she crouched with her maidens there. And she, too, saw him, and sprang to her feet though those with her would have restrained her. But with their arms about her she still stood and waved her hand to him and called, though he could not hear her words. Farther, farther, until he could no longer distinguish the dear form that had been taken from him.

He was borne back to his couch. They tried to cheer him ; but fiercely he waved them away.   He would be alone.

As he lay there, bowed with his grief, he felt a hand laid on his shoulder, and starting up, he saw the old monk, the head of that little community, looking down compassionately on him.

"Ah!   My son," said the monk, "I am old and have long since renounced the world and the things of this world ; but I, too, once was young and—I remember."

"Father," cried the prince, "none can ever have loved as she and I love."

The monk smiled sadly.   "That is ever the belief of all true lovers.   But of this I am assured—that love which is true and pure is of God and can never die."

Something in the old man's voice caused the prince to gaze at the face bent above him : but whatever he saw there, he forebore to speak.

"I go to pray for you both," the monk added, and, turning aside, he slowly paced towards the chapel.

Days passed, and nights in which the prince lay sleepless, or slept but to dream troubled dreams in which Thyra's face seemed to look on him with appealing eyes, and he thought he heard her calling in distress, calling him to come.   Waking, trembling, he would start up

in the darkness, and he, too, would call, call
aloud her name, and listen for an answer that
never came.

At length, his longing for her growing
intolerable, he bade his men prepare
a boat for him, determining that he himself
would cross to the mainland, and there ascend
a high hill that thence he might the better
watch for his lady's return ; nor would he be
dissuaded from his purpose though the monks
added their remonstrances to the entreaties
of his own men. Only one concession he made
—that he would delay his journey until they
should have satisfied themselves that Red
Hector of the hills and his followers were not
lying in wait for him. But when those who
were sent to make this investigation returned
with the tidings that the bandit could be heard
of nowhere, nothing would deter the prince
from setting forth.

He was rowed across accordingly with two
of his retainers, and with their assistance
painfully climbed to a point from which a
wide view could be obtained ; but not to the
summit of the hill, for that was beyond his
strength. He could see the far receding
waters of the loch, the undulations of the hills,
and the pass by which travellers from the west
must approach ; but though he sat there day
after day, silently keeping vigil, his patience

was unrewarded. Hardly to any would he speak and he ate but little. His men, with anxiety, saw that his cheeks grew paler, his form more wasted, and that his strength, which, while the princess had been with him, he was rapidly regaining, was now ebbing. His whole mind seemed to be overshadowed by melancholy.

The old monk watched him with troubled eyes. " My son," he reasoned, " it is not thus that you will serve the lady of your love should she need your aid. You waste your strength and life.

" Of what avail is my life to me," the prince answered bitterly, " when I know well that I shall never see her face again in this world."

One day, when scarcely had he been able to reach his accustomed watching place on the brow of the hill, so enfeebled was he, the sky which at first had been clear was gradually overcast and drifting mists obscured the hills. Soon, so densely did these vapours enfold them that neither he nor his men could see farther than a few feet ahead. As they could serve no purpose by remaining, they therefore decided to return ; but, familiar though the way had seemed when all was clearly to be seen, somehow they strayed, sometimes floundering into deep pools of peaty water, or forcing a difficult way through entanglements of bracken. It was with relief, therefore, that they suddenly encountered a man.

They saw him sitting on a stone, and at first, as his form loomed through the mist, he seemed to be of gigantic proportions ; but on closer approach that illusion was dispelled. He was apparently old, infirm, and poor. His bonnet was drawn over his face, the lower part of which was hidden beneath a long, white beard. White, too, was the hair which strayed over his ears and neck. A threadbare cloak was thrown around him, and he leaned his head upon his hands, clasping a staff.

The prince greeted him, "Who, and what are you ? " he asked.

"My name is Dugald, and I am of the MacKenzie clan," the old man answered in trembling, muffled tones. "But what I shall be, ask of the ravens, ask of the eagles, not of me."

"What mean you by that, friend ? " the prince, much perplexed, enquired.

The other rocked himself to and fro. "Woe, woe is me ! " he wailed. "Homeless, friendless, poor, and old, what is there left for me but to leave my carcase on the hill-side ? "

Seeing one, who, like himself, seemed to be plunged in misery, the prince, who was ever gentle and courteous to the aged, and more so when to age was added distress, demanded whether he had indeed no home or friends, and the reason for this destitution.

"Until yesterday no man was more content than I," answered Dugald, "I had wife and son and cattle. To-day wife and son are dead, and my cattle taken from me."

Deeply moved, the prince asked how this terrible calamity had befallen.

Sudden rage seemed to shake the old man where he sat. His hands tightened on his staff, and his utterance was choked as he answered : "The black curse rest on him and his. May fever waste and famine gnaw him to the bone. May he look for grace and find none in the face of friend or foe, in earth or heaven."

"Of whom speak you ? "

"I speak of Red Hector of the hills."

"Ah," cried the prince, "I, too, have a reckoning with him. What has he done to you ? "

"Every beast that I had he has taken from me. My son he has slain. And my wife, in the madness of her grief, flung herself into the loch and is drowned. I have nothing left and were better dead."

"Nay," corrected the prince, "for you have revenge left still."

"Revenge," the other repeated, "what hope of revenge is left to me—old, stricken,

and feeble as I am ?   Were the young blood
of my manhood yet hot in my veins then, indeed, revenge might be mine ; but not now."

"Be not so sure of that. Cannot your
wrongs be avenged by another ?   I, too, have
suffered at the hands of Red Hector of the hills,
and have vowed that, if I live, he shall answer
for his villainy."

"Ha !" cried Dugald, "then it may be I
can serve you and my own purpose in one."

"How so ?"

"None knows Red Hector better than I.
His hiding places are familiar to me.   I shall
know when he returns.   Let me serve you, and
old and feeble though I be, the time will come
when I shall deliver him to you."

With this proposal the prince concurred.
And so it was with old Dugald as a guide that
they retraced their way to the boat ; but
further he would not go ; only promising to
meet the prince at the same spot daily, and
that meanwhile he would keep watch against
the return of the man whom both abhorred.

Next morning the prince met Dugald at the
place appointed, and together they climbed
the hill.   Both seemed preoccupied with their
thoughts and sat silently. But after a time
the prince turned towards his companion.
"You have told me of yourself," he said ;
"but you have asked nothing concerning me."

From beneath the dingy tangle of his disordered hair and brows the old Highlander's eyes lowered ominously on the young man before him. " It may be that I know more of you than you suppose," he answered.

" What do you know of me ? "

The other continued to gaze fixedly as if in a trance. He answered slowly : " I see a fair ship, with white sails set, which sails to bear you over a wide sea to where a kingly crown awaits you.   And all that royal heritage you would lay at the feet of the one you love."

" A   ship ! "   cried   the   prince,   " You see that— ? "

" That, and much more."

" You are a seer ? "

" To me is given, at times, the power of vision."

" What else do you see ? "

" I see a people of another land who mourn and weep, and I hear their cry of sorrow. From the shadows of mourning I see arise the pale face of one who is very fair.   She dreams of you."   He paused.

The prince eagerly seized his arm. " More, tell me more," he urged.

But the seer shook off the hand that grasped him.   " Touch me not," he bade.   "The vision fades."

From that day onwards and for many days

the prince was attended by his newly-found
guide ; though his own personal followers
were much opposed to the innovation.   They
disliked and mistrusted the newcomer, and
indeed, there was something strange and
disquieting in his stealthy demeanour and
malevolent looks. But their master would
listen to none of their protests ; often dismiss-
ing those tried and faithful friends that he
and the sinister old man might be alone
together. Side by side they would sit, far
up the shoulder of the hill, and look out westward to the pass by which travellers from that
direction must approach. And often to those
watching them, yet too distant to hear their
whispered words, it would be evident that in
prophetic trance Dugald held his listener
spellbound. What was said on these occasions
was never made known ; only the prince's
dejected bearing and wasting strength bore
evidence of melancholy forebodings ; yet, so
potent was the hold which the other laid on
him that he seemed unable to free himself
from this tyranny of depression. His friends
found, at least, some comfort in the reflection
that no word reached them of the return of
Red Hector of the hills.

At length a day came when the prince was
so enfeebled that only by vehement commands
and threats could he prevail upon his men to

bear him to the boat.   The truth of the matter was that the wound in his side had broken out again, but he concealed the fact from them, bidding them support him, though the pain which he endured was great.   As was usual on these occasions, they found the old Highlander awaiting them on the further shore. He seemed to be in great agitation, urging the prince to disembark with all haste.   But the prince, despite his utmost efforts, was wholly unable to proceed.

Seeing his distress, Dugald approached and whispered in his ear that he should bid his men stand aside, and that order having been given and obeyed, " Listen," he whispered, " I have dreamed of a great army of her kingdom on their way hither, but a shadow, as of death, hung over them.   To-morrow we should know what this portends."

" To-morrow," the prince repeated, " I cannot wait until to-morrow."

" Hush ! " the Highlander bade him. "Dismiss your men, and I shall convey you that you may meet her if she be yet alive."

" Go," cried the prince to his followers, " leave me here, and to-morrow return for me."

They expostulated ; but all in vain.   With Dugald's arm around him he turned away ; but he had not taken many steps before his head sank upon his breast, and he fell fainting to the ground.

Still unconscious, they carried him to the boat; but before they could push out, he revived and bade them stay. He beckoned Dugald to his side. "Go alone," he commanded, "since I cannot accompany you. Go with all the haste you may. Tell her that I await her as the drowning man awaits the hand that succours him. And come again and tell me whether all be well. Recall the strength of youth and speed as an arrow speeds; then ask for what reward you will and it shall be yours."

"I shall do your bidding," answered Dugald, "and before noon to-morrow I shall return. See yonder hill on the horizon;" he pointed. "I shall signal from that point. If all be well you shall see a red flame leap upward, but if ill, then a black smoke only shall ascend."

"But if I see black smoke, how shall I know what evil has befallen?"

"The black smoke shall ascend only if the worst have befallen and she be dead."

"Angels and Saints defend her!" cried the prince; "but I vow to God that if she be dead, then shall my life also end."

At these impassioned words Dugald looked darkly at him; but spoke no word, and next moment, turning aside, he hastened away.

All that night the prince sat alone in the pale moonlight which streamed through his open window. He watched the quivering beams of moon and stars play on the rippling waters of the loch, and glitter like silver on a thousand springs which trickled from the moss and fern of the hills. He heard the sigh of the wind in the trees and the melancholy cry of night birds. And his fear, aroused by the old man's ominous vision, overshadowing him like the night, was yet lit by the sweet starlight of his hope that on the morrow the dear face of his lady might smile on him again, and that his sighs might be silenced by the glad singing of his heart with her return. He recalled his first meeting with her, not so long passed, and yet life until that moment seemed to him now to have been but an empty dream. He could live only in her presence. Every word she had spoken, her every look he had treasured in his heart, and now recalled them fondly as a miser counts his gold. He tried to picture her as she might be at that moment. Was she asleep ? Did she dream of him ? And in her dreams was her spirit near him ? "Thyra, Thyra," he whispered her name. But he heard only the restless leaves stirring as the breath of night troubled their slumber, and the long ripples lapping on the shore. Not until the eastern sky was gray with coming dawn did he, exhausted, fall asleep.

Not long after daybreak the door of his room opened very softly, and the old monk stole within. He stood looking down silently, with pity in his eyes, on the wasted, recumbent form, and, turning again, would have withdrawn without waking the sleeper, but the prince looked up and, for a moment seemed to gaze without recognition on the intruder.

"It is I, my son." the monk reassured him. "I came to see how you fared."

"I fare well, Father," the prince smiled, "since this is the day that brings my lady back to me. See, the sun shines on a prosperous world."

"And yet not thus should you have prepared for her coming, my son. You are sick and should rest on your couch."

"Nay," cried the prince, "all things awake to greet her with laughter, and shall not I?" And he arose to his feet, but the pain of his re-opened wound caused him to stagger, and he would have fallen had not the other caught him; nor did he reveal his suffering or its cause; but strove to make light of the old man's anxiety on his behalf.

Though he insisted on leaving the dwelling, no efforts could prevail to carry him far, and he had soon to sink for rest on a bank from which a wide view of the loch extended westward. Here he could watch for any signal

which might herald the approach of the
princess and her train. The anxieties which
had haunted him on the previous night, and
indeed for many days, all seemed now banished
from his mind, and though his face was still
pale, yet now it was illuminated with a wonderful brightness of expectant happiness. His
pain seemed all forgot, and he laughed gaily
with those who came about him. No doubt
seemed to cross his mind that Thyra would
come ere many hours had passed, and that,
reunited, life and joy extended radiantly
before them forever.

Seeing the gaiety of his spirits in such striking contrast to the black despair in which he
had been plunged, his followers were greatly
relieved, but the old monk, narrowly observing
him, shook his head ; so had he seen the fickle
sunshine before a storm.

All morning the prince sat there, waiting for
her in vain. They brought him food and
drink ; but little of these he would take. He
seemed upborne by a strength apart from his
body and its needs. The noon of a glorious
day passed, and still he watched. Sundown
at length and the glories of a sunset in crimson
and gold over the hills. Blood-red the waters
glowed beneath. They were watching with
him now, monks and men, standing in groups,
a little back from where he sat. For a

time none had spoken. Strange silence fell
on all around. They almost held their
breath. And still that wondrous pageantry
of the ever-changing sky unfolded over a land
which seemed enchanted in its mystery of
dimly receding mountain and glen. Far off one
huge shoulder arose shadowing the light and
suddenly from its summit trailed a thin,
wavering spiral of smoke, upward it curled,
gradually increased in volume until it strayed,
a column black as death, against the sky.

With white, set face and eyes fixed on that
dreaded signal, of which none but he had been
forewarned, the prince slowly arose and stood
rigid. He spoke never a word. They stared
at him in wonder, but forebore to question.
Minutes passed.

Suddenly, "See! See!" cried one, and
pointed.

Straining their gaze, they saw three dark
shapes glide into view, the flash of oars and
they knew that great galleys sped over the
waters. From one a flag floated and they
recognised it as the royal flag of Ulster.

"She comes, she comes!" they cried, and
turned towards the prince expecting to see him
in transports of joy; but he stood unmoved,
still silent.

The old monk hastened to him. "My son,"
he said, with great emotion, "God has heard

F

our prayers and those of the blessed Saints for you. Let us go and prepare for her and those with her."

But the prince did not reply.

The old man turned to give directions to his subordinates ; then stretched a hand towards the prince. "Will you not come ?" he asked. Afterwards he recalled the look in the stricken man's eyes—a strange look, as if he gazed on a world unseen. But at the moment the good father paid no heed. Only he paused.

"She awaits me," at length answered the prince, and smiled.

"Nay, rather, we await her."

"In the chapel," he spoke as in a dream "in the chapel where she said that we should wed. I go to meet my bride."

Supposing that the lovers had pledged themselves to meet at their re-union in that holy place, the monk, wondering a little, was yet reluctant to upset so pious a resolve, and so, summoning the others, he hastened away.

None marked the solitary form which with faltering steps, unseeing eyes, and hands out-held as if to enfold one whom he blindly sought, passed slowly within the chapel door.

*   *   *   *   *   *

On the shore monks and attendants assembled to welcome the approaching galleys. Very swiftly these great boats ploughed through the waters of the loch, sending the spray leaping from their prows and leaving long, troubled furrows trailing behind as the oarsmen bent to their task. The largest of these craft led the way, and on her prow stood a mail-clad soldier holding a staff from which a flag floated.

He hailed the group of watchers on the shore, and was answered by their shout of greeting. These were the galleys of MacKenzie, and many of that clan mingled with the men of Ulster whom they aided. The standard bearer, who was also leader of these strangers, was the first to leap into the shallow water. Others followed who drew the vessel upward on the beach, while he stood with uplifted arms. And then those on the shore saw her arise— Thyra, as a star arises from a cloud, or as the dawn awakens from the eastern sky. So in her pale beauty she cast aside her cloak and stood for a moment looking eagerly towards the island, scanning the faces of those assembled there, searching for one beloved. Then she was borne ashore.

She knelt as the old monk blessed her, and then, arising, " Father," she cried, " is all well ? "

" All is well, my daughter. He whom you seek awaits you in the chapel. I shall myself take you to him."

But she asked that she might go alone. And so, alone, she passed through those who thronged about her, bidding them see rather to the welfare of her escort. Thus they let her go, and did not observe the crouching form which slipped from the crowd and stealthily followed after her.

With tumult in her breast Thyra flew to the chapel, but paused for a moment by the open door. He was within. Her heart told her that. Why had he not met her ? And yet, he was right ; sweeter that he and she should meet alone with none to see, here where they were to be wed. Should she whisper his name, whisper that she had come ? No, rather she would steal upon him unawares ? With smiling lips she crossed the threshold and looked within. Silence, darkness—save that a narrow shaft of light fell dimly on the altar. For a moment she stood motionless, breathless, looking around. In sudden fear she called loudly. None answered. Then she saw him, lying outstretched before the altar on the stone-paved floor, his face upon his arm. Panic-stricken, with choking breath, she rushed to him, flung herself kneeling by his side, clutching his hand. It was cold and stiff. He was dead. A heart-broken cry rang from her lips as she fell beside him. And all her world, which a moment before had appeared so full of joy, seemed now to crash in ruins around her It could not be true. He could not be dead. She must control her trembling limbs, must seek for help, summon assistance. She struggled upright to find the old man, Dugald, looking down on her. "Help me," she appealed, "something terrible has happened."

He stooped, laid a hand for a moment on the fallen man's heart. "He is dead," he told her.

"No, no," she wailed, "it cannot be so. Not dead ; not dead."

"He is dead," he repeated.

"O, God!" she cried in bitter distress.

But Dugald stood immovable, and never for an instant did his eyes waver from her face. "You cannot have loved a weak stripling such as he," he said.

"I loved him better than my life," she returned passionately.

He laughed mockingly.

"Who are you who come to taunt me in my grief ? " she demanded.

Suddenly the seemingly old man flung aside the cloak which had covered him, tore the disguise from his face, and revealed to her astonished and terrified gaze the dreaded features of Red Hector of the hills. "Yes," he laughed again, "you know me now."

"Red Hector," she exclaimed. "What do you seek here?"

In a single stride he stood above her while she cowered beneath. "What do I seek?" he repeated. "I seek you; for I love you a thousand times more than ever could that boy. I love you as a man should love a woman—accepting no denial, sweeping aside all who would oppose him from his path. I have come to take you to myself."

With all the intensity of her soul she looked into his eyes, and whispered, "I hate you."

"What care I for your hate?" he mocked. "Your hate will turn to love when you own me as your master!"

Slowly, still with her eyes on his eyes, she arose and looked him face to face. "There is not one hair of that dear head which lies there so low that I would give to save your soul from everlasting torment. I love him, and him only shall I love to all eternity."

"You dare to defy me?"

"I do not fear you—you who, were he alive, would never dare to show your face in his presence."

Madness seemed to possess the man who stood before her, madness flamed in his eyes, and blood flecked his lips as he gnawed them. "Listen then," he bade. "It was I who killed him. I who gave the signal which

told him you were dead. He died believing
he would never see you more."

" O vile, accursed coward ! " she choked
in her despair. " But you, too, shall suffer.
My men are without and shall seize you here
and now." She drew her breath to shriek
for help ; but, like a flash, he snatched his
dirk, and in an instant had plunged it deep
into her breast. She reeled from the blow,
and, sobbing, fell upon the floor.

Slowly the fire of insanity faded from his
face, giving place to horror as, for a few
moments, he stood still, looking at her lying
there. He glanced at his reeking dirk and
flung it from him, as a guilty thing, unfit again
for a man to use. Stealthily he turned and crept
softly away, like a hunted beast, to escape
to the hills whence he came.

Painfully, painfully, she drew herself until
she lay beside her dead lover. She stooped
and kissed his brow. " Stay for me," she
whispered. " I come, I come quickly," and
then she died.

*   *   *   *   *   *

" *Beati, beati, mortui*"—Blessed are the
dead. The voices of the monks assembled,
rose in mournful cadence. They were singing
the vespers of the dead. Before the altar

still the lovers lay; but now in everlasting peace, wedded, even as in her vision Thyra had foreseen, beautiful still as in life they had ever been. "*Beati, mortui.*"

Without, the sun had set, and twilight had fallen on a world stilled for sleep, not a breath stirred the leaves of the slender birches or stirred the bracken on the hills. From the quiet waters of the loch, mists floated, illuminated by the fading glory of the western sky as the monks at length filed slowly, with downcast eyes, from the chapel.

"Look, brother!" cried one, pointing: "Look yonder!"

"That is strange," the other answered.

And strange was the illusion which they saw, for by some unusual refraction of the twilight rays upon the mist, the vapours, far on the bosom of the waters, had assumed the form of a ship with white sails set, which seemed to sail into the splendour of a world of dreams.

EWEN AND HIS SEAL WIFE.

Cha d' thug gaol luath
Nach d' thug fuath clis.
Quick to love, quick to hate.

AH, the sweet, sad music that he sang! That was the strangest thing about Ewen. He might not be quite canny; indeed how could a man who would have nothing to do with his neighbours, preferring to sit in solitude, be quite sound in mind? But when he sat at sunset, out there where the great rocks stand guard around Seal Bay, and the sea was still, save where it lifted caressingly the trailing tangle and toyed with it as might a lover with the tresses of his loved one's hair, and the flitting sea-birds had ceased their plaintive cry, and all was hushed in the shadow of the coming night; then those who had the courage or curiosity to spy upon him, stealing from knoll to knoll and peeping from behind the rocks, would hear Ewen sing his sad, sad song that to all seemed beautiful, but which none could understand, for it was in no tongue known to his hearers.

Hector, the tacksman of Coll, had brought him from North Uist one day at Ewen's own earnest request. Hector had been charged with a mission to the distant island by his laird, and, about to return, had met Ewen and been implored by him to take him away. He would give no reason for his request except that great sorrow had overtaken him and he wished to see his native island no more. He could fish, he could mend boats—none better than he, he would faithfully repay with his services the refuge of a new home. If not— he could be cast out.

And so Hector the tacksman, staring for a time in doubt at the pale face of the suppliant with its wide, imploring eyes, gray as a clouded sea, had, on a sudden impulse of pity, granted the appeal and Ewen had sailed with him away.

By the Bay of Seals the stranger had built himself a little hut of stones and turf, thatched with rushes, and there he dwelt alone. Many kindly folk would, at first, have befriended him ; but, though he was never discourteous, he was reserved and silent and seemed to prefer solitude. And so, after a time, his evident wishes were respected and he was left in peace.

There was one exception to this rule : from the first day of his coming, Sheila, the tacksman's daughter, had noted the beauty of Ewen's face and the memory of it haunted her.

She herself was beautiful, with dark flashing eyes and lips as red as rowan berries. And these lips smiled not unkindly at Ewen. Every morning he, faithful to his promise, brought fish to the tacksman's house, often when other fishermen had empty nets and profitless lines ; for never was there a more skilful fisherman than he. And always Sheila was there to receive him with her smile and a look from beneath her long black lashes. But Ewen would stand with downcast eyes and answer her greeting with hardly a word.

Little thought, you may be sure, had Hector, her father, of whither his daughter's fancy had roamed ; for a very proud man indeed was Hector and near of kin to the laird himself. Very angry would he have been had he known that Sheila, for whom he had great ambitions, was favouring in her thoughts a poor unknown stranger such as Ewen. But Sheila was careful to retain her secret and was so cunning that in her father's hearing she often spoke lightly of Ewen, so that the tacksman had no suspicion of the truth of the matter.

Nevertheless she continued to meet the stranger every day and often, on some pretext or another, even by his solitary hut. Once she came limping to him as he sat by his door mending his nets, and, weeping, told him that while passing near she had wrenched her ankle and must seek his aid. He looked at her pityingly with his great, dreamy eyes; but it was in silence that he bound up the injured joint.

"I think Ewen," she said, "that there is a very bonny sweetheart that you will have left behind you in Uist."

"No," he answered, without looking up, "there is no maid in Uist that I love."

"Perhaps you have found one here?"

"You are the only maid here that I have spoken to."

"You are not one who cares for bonny maids?"

"I love all things that are beautiful."

"Look at me then, Ewen," she bade, and laid a light touch for a moment on his silky brown hair. "Look at me and tell me whether you think me bonny."

He looked as he was bidden. "I think," he answered, "you are the bonniest maid in all the island of Coll."

Her eyes met his sad eyes, provocative, alluring; but after a moment he bent his gaze again on the bandage which he wound around her ankle and added no word.

Suddenly she sprang to her feet, and, apparently quite forgetful of her injury, flounced from him and ran with never a backward look, leaving him still kneeling, staring open-eyed after her.

But Sheila was not convinced that she had no rival in her siege upon Ewen's heart. And as her failure continued she became deeply suspicious of him and determined to keep watch. So it was that for the first time she overheard his singing.

Ewen had hurried homewards one morning from Hector's house even more abruptly than was his wont. Why? Had he a tryst to keep? Sheila determined to find out for herself and so, making excuse to her father, after a little delay she followed Ewen. Gray mists hung heavy over the bleak, boulder-strewn hills, blotting out the landscape, drifting in wreaths over sea and shore, suiting her purpose; she could spy upon him, herself unseen. Wrapped in her plaid, swift and stealthy, she sped by familiar paths, pausing to listen here and there; then on again, until the sand was beneath her feet, the wash of the waves in her ears and she knew that Ewen's house must be near. But so dense was the mist that she could not be certain how far she had still to proceed before she should reach the dwelling. She was looking around for some landmark to guide her when she heard it—a voice that floated from the vapours in one long, plaintive call of strange sweetness, lingered a moment and died away ; only to awaken again and soar in liquid sounds and inarticulate music to silence once more.

She caught her breath, amazed, listening. And then the call was answered. Somewhere from the sea another voice arose and sang like wandering strains of wordless music. And yet, somehow she knew there was meaning in it. It seemed almost to reveal the secrets of the sea. Who called and was thus answered ? She must know. And so breathlessly she ran on and within fifty paces nearly fell over Ewen seated on a rock, the tide flowing at his feet.

"What do you seek here ? " he asked coldly, turning angry eyes on her.

"I was listening to your song," she answered.

"Well then, since you have heard it, there will be no need for you to stay."

"Indeed no. And for a man who has no sweetheart, it was a very pretty answer that some maid in a boat out yonder (she tossed a hand seaward) would be singing to you."

"You are mistaken, however," he told her.

"It is very likely that I have been mistaken in taking notice of a worthless fisherman like you ; so I shall leave you and your sweetheart." She flung her retort at him and turning rushed blindly into the mist again. Only when she was far up the hillside and secure from all observation did she throw herself sobbing on the drenching heather. But from that hour Sheila sought revenge on the man who had slighted her advances, and first she tried to poison the mind of her father against him. She had, however, to be very wary ; it would never do if Hector were to be informed of the visits she had made to Ewen's hut.

"He is a rude man," she denounced.

"There is no need for you to have anything to do with him," returned her father.

"I am thinking he would be better back in Uist."

"He is more useful to me here," was Hector's opinion concerning the most skilful fisherman on the island.

And so for a time Sheila's schemes were thwarted ; but it was, perhaps, from hints and covert insinuations dropped by her that strange rumours as to the solitary fisherman became current amongst the folk of Coll. Perhaps he was not so solitary as he seemed. They heard and marvelled at the sweetness of his singing ; but on misty days, or when twilight faded to dusk, or in the gray of early dawn, there was one—even as Sheila had heard —who sang unseen, but as mysteriously and as sweetly as he, in answer to him. Could it be that one of his own people whom he had left

behind was seeking him here, urging him homeward again ?   Or was the singer from the sea
an elle-maid charming him from the world
of men ?   Better, perhaps, to leave this man
to his solitude.   And so Ewen was left more
and more alone.

Now, about half a mile inland from the Seal
Bay, where Ewen's hut had been built, is a
loch, known as the ' Loch of the Strangers,'
and on it is a little islet called ' Olaf's Isle.'
It had been in days of old the stronghold of a
Lochliner* ; but for many years the dwelling-
place had been allowed to crumble in ruins.
Still, however, it was not so decayed as to be
beyond repair, and the causeway which
connected the island-fort with the mainland
was still in being.   For long all had been
neglected, unoccupied, and therefore great
was the surprise of Hector the tacksman,
when one day Ewen asked if he might live on
Olaf's Isle.

"And why would you be wanting to do
that ? " asked Hector.

" I want it for my wife," answered Ewen.

" Your wife !   I did not know that you had
one."

" Oh, yes indeed," Ewen affirmed, " I have
still a wife, though she left me and I never

* A Norse Viking.

thought to see her again. But now, one day she will return."

" Have you had news of her ? "

" Yes, I have had news of her."

Hector was much mystified. " Very well, Ewen," he at length agreed. " I shall tell the laird of your request and, if he offers no objection, you may live on Olaf's Isle ; though indeed it is a strange place you choose for your wife and you to live in."

And so, for some days after his interview with Hector, Ewen was seen to be at work on Olaf's Isle, repairing the ruined dwelling, thatching the roof, hanging a new door on its hinges and making all habitable. But no one had as yet seen anything of his wife either at his old home or at the new.

About a week had passed and a sultry day had ended in a severe thunderstorm. Rain and wind raged violently over the island and lashed the sea to a fury of tempestuous waves. It was not a night when any living creature who could find shelter would choose to be without. Nevertheless, Hector the tacksman rode abroad. He had had business to transact at a distant part of the island and was urging his horse homeward with all speed, bending forward beneath the storm, his bonnet drawn well over his face, when suddenly the horse shied, all but unseating Hector, who,

G

looking up, could just discern before him in the darkness a black form which seemed that of a man heavily burdened. "Who are you?" shouted Hector angrily, for he had barely escaped a fall.

"It is Ewen, the fisherman, that is very sorry for frightening his honour," came the answer.

"And what might you be doing here on such a night as this?" demanded Hector, recollecting, however, as he spoke that he was not far from Ewen's hut by the sea.

"It is my wife that has come back to me and I carry her to our new home."

"If your wife, has come in safety to Coll on such a night as this, then I think she must be more fish than woman. But stand now aside and let me pass, for I have no mind to delay." And Hector spurred on his way leaving Ewen to toil onwards with his burden.

Weeks passed, and though Ewen brought his fish as usual to the tacksman's house, he never again encountered Sheila there, nor did he ever speak to anyone of the wife whom he had taken to his new home. But there were those who saw her, never close at hand, for she always fled at the approach of strangers; but from a distance they spied on her and all agreed that she was the loveliest woman they had ever beheld. She had long brown hair and often she could be seen sitting on the causeway, dangling her white feet in the water of the loch and combing her long tresses. There were those, too, who declared that they had heard her sing just such sweet mysterious music as had been heard previously from the sea. But that report Hector never would believe, affirming that the woman was dumb.

The tacksman had formed this conclusion because he alone had been successful in approaching Ewen's wife. One day he had occasion to ride by the Loch of the Strangers and did so more readily in the hope of himself catching a glimpse of the beautiful woman about whom so many were talking. He was more successful than he had dared to hope. Though the sun shone brightly a high wind blew, thus carrying from the woman the sound of Hector's approach until the horse was almost upon her. She had strayed a little further than was her wont and was sitting on a rock beneath which the loch lay deep and dark. She sprang instantly to her feet and with a muffled cry would have fled ; but Hector was too quick for her. He flung himself from his horse and caught the loose, flying garment with which only she seemed to be arrayed. She cowered at his feet and upraised wide eyes of terror to his face ; but she spoke no word.

For a moment Hector stared in astonishment at the beauty of her face; then he smiled not unkindly. "You need not flee from me, lassie," he sought to reassure her. "I would be loath to hurt one as bonny as you."

Still she spoke no word.

"I would only know whether all is well with you in that queer home that Ewen has made for you there. You must know that I am the laird's cousin and am tacksman on this island."

Still silence.

Hector was puzzled. "Can you understand me, lassie?" he asked.

She laid a finger on her lips and shook her head.

Then he knew that she was dumb and at once, in pity for her infirmity and agitation, he released his hold on her garment. In a moment she had rushed from him to the end of the ledge of rock, and, ere he could raise a hand to detain her, plunged in with a great splash and sank from his sight.

Horror-struck he stared at the heaving waters, ready to stretch a hand to her when she should reappear; but he waited in vain, in agony of mind, gazing with starting eyes at the loch which quickly smoothed out its broken surface and mirrored again the bright sky above. He was about to dive in the hope of

still recovering her when something far off
caught his attention. What was that? Yes,
surely it was she! Her face above the water,
watching him! Like a wild-duck, she had
swum submerged, until fifty yards separated
them; then she had arisen and was watching
him there. He had not known that a human
being could swim like that. In any case he
need have no fear lest she should drown. Half
relieved and half angry to have been so needlessly disturbed, he remounted his horse and
rode away.

Of course all these strange stories were
repeated to Sheila; but she seemed to pay
little heed to them. It was of no interest to
her, she declared, what Ewen the fisherman
did, or with whom he chose to live. She for
one would not believe that the woman was his
wife.

"But who then is the lassie?" asked
Hector.

"Oh," Sheila answered, "a day will come
when you will know who and what this woman
is whom you permit to live in Coll."

"Ah, well," sighed the tacksman, "all
I now know is that the poor lass is sorely
afflicted and a fairer than she I have certainly
never seen."

Meanwhile Sheila, for some reason or
another, became very pale of face and her

eyes were often red as from weeping, though none ever saw her shed tears. And though she had declared indifference to Ewen and his wife, perhaps Hector's daughter was more interested in them than she would have had her father believe ; else why did she one day seek counsel of old Donald ?

The old man was very wise and well known as a seer. So to Donald Sheila went one day and told him that she greatly feared for her father and indeed for all the folk of the island, because there had come into their midst one who was, she felt sure, an elle-maid who would bring great misfortune to them.

Long and earnestly Donald gazed at the sheep shoulder-blade on his knee, mumbling while he traced with one bony finger the marks of divination which he saw there. " You are mistaken, Sheila," he at length told her. " She is no elle-maid who has come to this island from the sea."

" What then ? "

" Tell me first what you know concerning the man ; for woeful things seem to be unfolded to my sight, things that were better for you should not be. Tell me what you know of the man."

" I know little of him except that he came from Uist."

" And his clan ? "

" I have heard my father say that Ewen is of the Macodrums."*

Donald started at the mention of the name. " Listen ! " he bade. " It is as I thought : he himself is of the seal folk. Now I can tell you what you must do if you would banish this strange woman forever." And so, drawing the girl closer to him, he whispered secret instructions in her ear.

The next day the sun blazed fiercely as Sheila stole unseen from her father's house, and avoiding observation, made her way over the hills to the Loch of the Strangers. She knew that Ewen would be there ; for, some hours previously, he had brought his fish to the tacks-man and would not again seek the sea until dusk. But for a time not a soul was in sight— no sound or movement ; no ripple broke the surface of the loch. Only the hot air quivered over the heather. She saw the little islet with its newly repaired habitation ; but no ascending smoke told that its inmates were there. She must make certain of that. Very guardedly she advanced, creeping on hands and knees from hillock to hillock and from boulder to boulder until less than a hundred yards separated her from the causeway of stones piled laboriously by men of old so that

* The Macodrums were said to be descended from seals.

a narrow footway wound from the shore to the islet. And then, peeping from the heather, she saw them all unconscious of her approach. On a huge, sloping slab of rock by the water's edge they reclined together, basking in the sun. The woman sat, her long hair unbound, her garment clinging around her, but leaving white shoulders and arms bare ; while lying by her side, his head upon her breast, his arms enfolding her, was Ewen. Even at that distance Sheila could see the rapture in his face uplifted to the face he loved. And with teeth biting fiercely on her lip Sheila smothered the sob that arose from her aching heart ; and yet she could not avert her eyes. Ah, how happy they seemed, together there ! How lovely were both ! reclining in silence, content to be together, motionless saving for little caressing touches and slow, languid movements, luxuriating in the sunshine and in each other's love !

She could at length endure no more. With burning eyes and pale, set face Sheila turned aside, and, as secretly as she had come, she crept again away, until, beyond sight of the islet, she uprose and ran, ran with beating heart and panting breath, over the hills to the Bay of the Seals and to Ewen's abandoned hut. With one swift look around to make sure she was unseen she entered and looked. All was bare, save that

withered grass and heather strewed the earthen
floor and the charred ashes of a fire had been
left untouched. Soot hung from the rafters
and about the blackened hole in the centre
of the roof from which smoke had escaped.
No furniture remained. She kicked aside the
litter on the floor, searching for any indication
of recent digging ; but found none. She
felt the bare stones and turf of the walls.
None had of late been loosened to form a hiding
place for that which she sought. Her search
seemed fruitless ; but suddenly a thought
struck her and she hurried out again. Still
she was alone—not a soul was in sight. The
thatch ! It hung low, easily within her reach.
Feverishly now she made her way around,
prodding, groping and at length, with a sudden
gasp of satisfaction, found what she had known
must have been somewhere concealed—a large
bundle, carefully wrapped together. Quickly
she unwound it, spread it wide on the turf—
a sealskin more beautiful than any she had
ever seen, perfect, entire, white and soft as
the purest silk. All was well. Donald had
been right. Oh, how glad, glad she was that
she had been guided by his advice ! Now
she must be patient and bide her time. Nothing could be done until she was sure that Ewen
was out of the way, and that would not be
ere night had fallen and he engaged on his

fishing. Concealing again the sealskin in the thatch—she dared not risk its discovery by taking it with her—she returned to her home, there to await the close of day.

The long summer twilight had faded from the hills and valleys; pale stars twinkled overhead and flickered in reflected silver from the loch and a glorious moon flooded with magic light the earth and sea as Sheila glided noiselessly, herself like a shadow of the night, towards the Loch of the Strangers until within sight once more of Olaf's Isle. And there again she hid, keeping vigilant watch on the causeway. She had not long to wait. From the door of his abode she saw Ewen step forth, carrying his fishing nets and behind him came the woman he claimed as his wife. Perhaps she was indeed dumb; but if they spoke, Sheila was too far distant to overhear their words. Only he held his love long and tenderly, and, with many a backward glance and wave of his hand, picked his way over the causeway to the shore. For a moment or two the woman stood where he had left her, watching him; and then suddenly seemed swept by her love for him to his arms again; for she fled, light as driven foam, to his embrace once more. Then again they parted, and, though she followed him a little way by the loch side, she did not again overtake him;

but stood, beautiful in the moonlight, and looked as his form faded from her view. Even after many minutes had passed and he must have been far distant, she still stood, motionless.

Here was Sheila's opportunity. Swiftly, swiftly she stole while the other was thus engaged, raced towards the causeway, flung upon the gravel there the sealskin which she had recovered and then darted to concealment again, unseen. Minute after minute crept by. Very soon now Ewen would reach his boat on the sea shore and be gone. Would the woman stand there all night? She had turned at last and with slow, dejected pace and downcast looks was retracing her way homeward. Suddenly she saw the sealskin and stared at it for a time as if in bewilderment—as might one who strove to recall a memory. Then with a low, inarticulate cry she fell upon her knees and clasped the skin to her bosom, fondling it, caressing it as if it were a long lost treasure. And all the while she crooned and murmured to herself. So occupied was she that, for a moment or two, she did not observe Sheila who now advanced boldly, openly towards her ; but a shadow fell and the woman leaped to her feet, still clasping the skin and turning a terrified face to the intruder. For a breathless second they stood in silence, face to face ; then, quick as a flash, the woman darted for the causeway to escape ; but Sheila was quicker and barred her way.

A sort of cold, suppressed fury seemed to freeze the girl to calm ; for no tremor shook her voice. " You have got what you need," she said. " Now go."

There was no answer ; only the woman shrank from the blazing eyes bent upon her.

" Do you not understand ? " Sheila continued. " I tell you to go again to the sea from which you came." Her breath came quicker now. And then suddenly the ice of her suppression burst asunder from her rage. "I know what you are," she panted. "You are no woman at all. You are a monster, a monster in human form. You have come to steal a man by your horrible wiles ; but you shall not have him. You shall not take him from me ; for if you do not go I shall kill you." Menacingly, ruthlessly, as she spoke she advanced on her cowering rival.

For a second it seemed as if the woman were spell-bound, unable to move hand or foot. Then with a moan of terror she was up, and, still clasping the skin, fled like the wind away.

Sheila watched her go and a fierce, exulting sense of victory held her motionless. But she must see the end, the fulfilment of her triumph. Not a moment was to be lost. So she too ran swiftly, pursuing. She knew the course the hated being must have followed— by the side of a little burn, down to the sea but half a mile distant. Fleet of foot as a deer Sheila ran ; but could not overtake the other, could not even see her, clearly as the moonlight shone. From side to side of the stream she leaped as the banks offered footing, never pausing, on she sped until the sand was beneath her feet and before her lay the silvered waters of the sea stilled in the fulness of the tide. The great rocks arose far out, black as death. Not a whisper came from the waters. She paused, looking around her, listening—no sign of living creature, no sound. Suddenly her anger passed from her, giving place to fear. Trembling she looked on the sand, searching to and fro. Yes, they were there— faint prints of flying feet, leading to the sea and—what then ?

She must go home, at once, quickly. Turning, with bowed head, she ran blindly, not heeding whither she went, her heart beating to suffocation. And suddenly she shrieked aloud ; for a strong hand had caught her and she sank, looking upward to see Ewen's face bent over her.

Not yet embarked, from a distance he had seen her, and, in instinctive fear, had rushed to her. "My wife!" he cried. "Where is my wife?"

"Oh, Ewen," she sobbed, "forgive me, forgive me."

"What do you mean? What have I to forgive?"

She clasped his knees. "She was no woman, Ewen," she pleaded. "She was no woman, as I am. You could not love her."

"I love her better than my life."

"No, no, I will not believe it. She charmed you with her spells. She put her magic on you that she might take you away. And now she has gone forever."

"Gone! gone where?" he cried despairingly and broke from her embrace, looking wildly about him.

But Sheila did not answer and the serene loveliness of the night looked coldly, in impassive silence, on him, unperturbed.

And then came the answer to his cry—from the sea a call in strange, unearthly music, wonderful in mystery and sweetness, seeming to bid him come away, away from care and sorrow to a realm of peaceful dreams. To come away, to come away. . . .

Sheila heard it and raised her head, listening intently, gazing outward at the sea. What was that? Something out there, floating in the moonlight! A seal! surely a white seal! Just for a moment it appeared; the next was gone. She turned. "Ewen, Ewen!" she screamed; but he heeded her not. He was racing to the sea. She watched him reach the water and plunge in—his head, as he swam swiftly in the reflected glory, out, out, leaving a fleeting, glittering trail; still onwards, until, in the splendour of mingled sea and sky, he passed for ever from her sight.

DONALD GORM.

Is beo duine an deidh a shàrachadh,
Ach cha bheo e'n deidh a nàireachadh.

A man may live after being harassed,
But not after being disgraced.

MACLEOD of Dunvegan sat one winter's
night by the fire in the great hall of
his castle and listened to the wind as
it howled in the battlements overhead. All
alone he sat, for he had no wife or family
and few of his kinsmen or retainers sought his
company. But for the firelight the hall was
in darkness, so that, as the chief reclined in
his oaken settle, his shadow was cast, distorted
and leaping on the walls around him. Sometimes the wind roared angrily in the chimney,
sending outwards sudden gusts of smoke and
sparks ; sometimes it moaned as might a
lost soul. Then, for a space, silence would
reign and he would hear the thunder of the
waves as they burst in cataracts upon the
rocky coast without. And all the fury and
unrest of the elements found their counterpart in the storms of vengeful fury and hatred
which raged within his breast.

MacLeod was thinking of the days gone by. He pictured again the time, when as a boy he had roamed that coast or wandered among the hills on long summer evenings, when the skies were clear, and larks sprang singing from the heather, and the plaintive cry of the curlew came tremulously in the air, or gulls screamed as they wheeled about the cliffs. He saw himself as he had been, a happy child, and he saw, too, his dear companion of those days—his sister, beautiful as she had always been, with her golden ringlets and her eyes of speedwell blue. Lithe, too, for like the roe she would leap from rock to rock without fear. How he had loved her! But who had not loved her? Not a clansman but would have died for her—Flora. . . . . .

He thought of how he and she both would sit there on cold nights, by that selfsame hearth, at the feet of their father, while with his arms laid lovingly about them he would tell them tales of the battles which their clan had fought and won, until his own boyish heart would thrill with pride of that father and of their heroic race, and he longed for the time when he, too, might go forth armed as a man to war.

Happy days! He remembered how all three would sit, in the stern of his father's great galley while the brawny armed crew

H

plied the oars so that the foam flew from the prow, and long furrows trailed behind ; out to sea, until the towering hills and crags of his native island lay dim in the distance.

And yet, even then, in childhood, a faint foreshadow of the disaster which was to overtake them had once fallen. He could recall the day as if it had been yesterday. He and Flora had run away in childish escapade, all unknown, taken a boat and sailed it to a distant part of the coast in search of cormorants' eggs. All day they had clambered together, happy, forgetful of time, until tired he had cast himself upon the beach, and there had fallen asleep, leaving his sister to wander alone. He had been awakened by cries of distress, and leaping to his feet he had seen Flora hanging from a jagged point of rock above the incoming tide. Climbing rashly, alone, she had slipped and would have fallen into the sea had she not laid hold of that projecting spur of stone. She could not regain her footing. All she could do was to cling there, while beneath her the deep water heaved and clutched at her suspended, swaying form. He rushed to the rescue, tried to clamber on the face of the cliff to her aid ; but, miscalculating his footing, found himself at a stand-still, unable to advance. He was not then the strong swimmer he afterwards became. In his extremity he shouted and, to his amazement, an answering shout reached his ears. A boy stood on the beach below, from his dress and bearing, no common youth, waving his hand in reassurance. Without a moment's delay the newcomer dashed into the sea and, swimming powerfully, was just in time to seize the girl, as exhausted she fell into the waves. Retracing his way the young MacLeod had met the rescuer and the rescued on the beach, dripping, but unharmed. He knew now who the other was—Donald Gorm, son of MacDonald of Sleat. Even then he hated him, hated the half contemptous laugh with which the other had taunted him as he thanked him for saving his sister. He hated that Flora should permit the boy to stand with his arm still around her and that she should gaze, fascinated, as even then she seemed to be, by this handsome stranger. What right, after all, had he there? And yet it was impossible now, to demand an answer to that question. He was glad when the galley of the MacDonalds swept round the point to the shore, and Donald Gorm, ignoring him, but waving an adieu to Flora, had leapt on board and was borne from their view.

That had been the beginning of all the trouble that was to ensue. Flora had never forgotten the bold, handsome stranger. Even when they had ceased to be children, and she herself had become a lovely young woman, they met, sometimes in secret—that he guessed; sometimes openly. This intruder had even dared at times to come to Dunvegan Castle, and there had been courteously received by MacLeod, in spite of the warnings he (the chief's son) had given his father. The older man had seemed blind to the danger of permitting this friendship, himself beguiled by the plausible guest, unsuspicious of his danger. And so cunning had Donald Gorm been, that the sullen demeanour of the young MacLeod towards him had always been turned to the disadvantage of the latter. He had been made to appear churlish, and sullen, in contrast with the vivacity and impetuosity of the alluring visitor.

So events had been allowed to drift, until that fatal morning when a cry had rung throughout the castle announcing that Flora was nowhere to be found, had fled. Followed the wild and unavailing search—rumours of a boat which had been seen to glide at early dawn to the quay, and to the slender, plaided figure which awaited it there, and then swiftly, silently, with bent sail, off again. Tidings at length of the lovers, and of hasty marriage vows taken before some wandering priest. They had left the country, had gone none knew whither. Silence, as month followed month. A year, two years had passed. And then that night when she returned! Just such a night as this, with the wind howling around the battlements and cliffs, with waves which broke thunderously upon the shore. They had found her, alone but for one faithful attendant, at the castle gate— she, the daughter of MacLeod, crouching there as a beggar maid might crouch! He had cast her off. He had dared to insult her and her clan. Repudiating her marriage, he was about to wed the sister of MacKenzie of Kintail and she, his lawful wife, had returned in secret as she had fled, fearful for her life, her honour in the mire. Through that tempest she had come and now lay dying. For two days they nursed her, tending her with every care, but on the third the castle had echoed the loud wailing of the coronach for her death.

He was in hiding with his people, himself now their chief, he the traitor, the betrayer. Far and near the fiery cross was sped, summoning the clan MacLeod. They gathered in their battle array, vowing revenge. Terrible then was the face of MacLeod, as the thunder cloud from which falls the fiery bolt. Long and loud the shout with which his clansmen hailed their chief and his heir. Like a tossing forest of steel the claymores were brandished. Forward, forward!

And then, and then—disaster. By the chief, his father's side he had stridden, longing for the battle, confident of victory, while the pibroch rent the air. It was but a trailing heather root which had caught his foot ; but it sent him sprawling with a broken ankle on the ground. He had begged, implored, to be carried with them ; but by the chief's command he was borne away and he had watched the waving tartans as they vanished in the distance and listened until the last echo of the pipes had been lost amongst the hills. Then, as if a child again, he had wept tears of bitterness.

Waiting for the news of battle, here in this hall ; he whose long desired hour of revenge seemed to have come, only that it might be snatched away—waiting with the women, the children, and old men ; he whom all looked upon as the bravest of the brave. Would the long hours never pass ? Nothing but the mournful breaking of the long waves on the shore. Hour after hour, noonday, sunset, dusk. At length a shout borne on the wind, a clamour at the castle gate—the hall door burst open and the wild form of a clansman standing there, behind him an eager crowd pressing. Into the hall the man staggered, his head bare, the tangled hair about his face dripping with blood and sweat. Red Ian !

he knew him to be a runner swift as a deer.
He had brought tidings. Speak, speak!
What news! How his heart had seemed to
cease with a shock as the man suddenly flung
himself with a loud cry of despair at his feet
and gasped out his terrible story of rout and of
slaughter, defeat and flight from the Coolin
Hills; told in anguish how the chief had
rushed from his own men to strike down single
handed Donald Gorm, and how MacLeod had
been cunningly lured farther and ever farther
from support. Above the cliffs these two at
length had stood face to face; until, parrying
a blow from MacLeod's claymore, Donald
Gorm had leaped in and stabbed the other with
his dirk. Mortally wounded the chief reeled
from the blow. With yells his clansmen had
hacked their way to his succour—too late.
With giant strength Donald Gorm grappled
with the stricken man, wound his arms about
him and, heaving him bodily from the ground,
flung him from the precipice. Then with a
shout of defiance and derision he had fled.
Woe to that day of sorrow and of shame!

Himself now chief, how he had striven to
avenge his father's death, his sister's dishonour! None had ever questioned his
valour. He was acclaimed as the bravest of
all his gallant race. Challenge after challenge
he had sent to his enemy. The insolent

answer was always returned that Donald Gorm, and not he, would choose the day and hour of their meeting. He had sought to capture him ; but in vain. Again their clans had met in battle, and again his had lost the victory.

Three years now had passed since then, and revenge seemed as far off as ever. Day and night the thought had preyed on his mind, embittered his life, gnawed at his heart. He became a morose and solitary man, shunning the society of his kinsmen and, at length, shunned by them. Brooding continuously on his wrongs, he would sit by the fireside alone for hours, or wander by the seashore or on the hills.

Perhaps the violence of the storm this night had recalled memories of the past ; perhaps the uproar of the elements seemed to him to echo the tumult of emotions within his breast. Certainly these bygone scenes seemed to pass before him with extraordinary clarity. He could almost see his father standing before him there—a face which looked darkly, reproachfully on the son who had failed so long to revenge that father's death. Surely it was the shade of his sister that crouched —a little child shaken by a storm of grief, her face hidden in her hands, in sorrow for the shame which was to defile her later years— unavenged still unavenged.

He could endure no more. Starting to his feet with face uplifted and with clenched hands upheld he cursed his enemy. He cursed him living, and to all eternity. As if in answer to these fearful imprecations, a blast, louder than any that had blown, seemed to rock the very castle where it stood ; the flames of the fire were blown outward and a great cloud of smoke and sparks billowed from the chimney to the hall, obscuring for a few moments his view. As the rolling vapours slowly ascended to the ceiling, his heart leaped, for before him he saw what seemed to him the draped form of a woman. He had not seen her enter the hall ; he had not heard her approach. She was no member of his household ; of that he was sure. Something about her stirred the hair on his scalp and chilled his blood. He was afraid to look her in the face, and yet he must. And what a face ! It seemed to be continuously changing ; at one moment—that of a lovely child ; the next— the shrivelled, distorted features of a hag seemed to confront him. It was like a mirror before which an endless file of people of all ages and of all conditions paused for a moment to look. The form itself, too, seemed to waver like a shadow in a stream, to diminish as if retreating to remote distance, then again, slowly to increase, until it loomed above him, gigantic, appalling. And her voice when she spoke came sometimes as from afar, whispering softly, hardly audible ; and then again would swell in reverberating tones until it seemed to fill the hall with its thunder.

" Who and what are you ? " cried MacLeod.

" Who and what I am, it is not for you, MacLeod, to ask," she answered.

" Your name ? "

" I have no name that you would know."

" Why have you come here ? "

" To do your bidding."

" But why . . . . . ? I must know something of you. From whence have you come ? "

" Know this, that I have come from the shadows of the night, and from the shrieking of the gale. From the billows of the sea, I have arisen."

" Why do you come to me ? "

" Fierce rages the blast without, but fiercer still is the tempest of your hate, and darker than the night are the thoughts within your breast. To you I have come, for you have called me."

No air stirred within the hall, and yet MacLeod felt as if a hurricane raged around him, buffeting him, swaying him hither and thither. He gasped for breath, his heart beat almost to suffocation. But never yet had courage failed him and now, though Hell itself might threaten, he would still stand undaunted and face this fearful apparition. "Begone!" he cried. "There is nothing that you can do for me."

Next instant, as if blown by a mighty wind, she stood close before him, gazing with terrible eyes which seemed to pierce his soul. And then, as he still stood unflinching, "You lie," she shrilled. "Is there none whom you would not have borne to you? None whom you would not have delivered to your vengeance? Or if such an one there be, speak, and winds and waves shall do your bidding."

He staggered from her; for at her words the blood suddenly leaped within his chilled veins, and rushed tumultuously to his brow. "Donald Gorm!" he whispered hoarsely, "you can send me Donald Gorm!"

"He whom you name," she answered, "even now battles with the storm. I have bent unseen above his galley as it tosses on the sea. Say but the word, and the wind shall bear him to you."

"Go!" he shouted, "and, though Hell itself return with you, bring to me that man."

She laughed, and her laughter was as the scream of shingle torn backward by a retreating wave. "Wait!" she whispered. "There are first certain forfeits which you must pay."

"Take what you will, saving my life and

lands," he cried, "so that you deliver to me, Donald Gorm."

"Two things only I take from you," she answered. With eyes still fixed on his eyes she stood before him and slowly stretched a hand and arm, livid as those of one long drowned. She laid a finger on his breast. "Something I take from your heart," she said.

A chill as of ice struck through him and he trembled violently. But he spoke no word.

Again she stretched her hand and touched his brow, "and something from your mind," she added.

A cry of agony rang from MacLeod's lips, for now her touch was as fire. Flames seemed to whirl about him, scorching, bewildering. "No," he entreated, "no, not that, not that." He clasped his burning head within his hands, reeled blindly from her and fell fainting and unconscious to the floor.

When he awakened it was to find the arms of his faithful attendants around him. Gently, with loud exclamations of dismay they raised him and would have borne him to his bedchamber; but he thrust them from him and struggled to his feet. There was no need for their fears he told them—a passing faintness, that was all. But he drank the wine they offered. For a moment he stood, while his men still lingered near, trying to remember the vision he had seen ; but only vaguely could he recall to his mind the phantom form which had seemed to speak with him there.

Amongst those who had hastened to his aid were many of his near kinsmen, those who had known him intimately from his boyhood ; but never before had they seen the wild look which they now beheld in his eyes—like those of a hunted animal at bay. Never before had they seen his face haggard as it now was. For long he had shunned them, but still they would have shed the last drop of blood within their veins for him, chief as he was. But now, somehow, there was that about him from which they instinctively shrank, something which they dreaded. And yet, as never before, he clung to them, and would not let them go, and all the while his gaze strayed hither and thither, as if fearfully searching for what they could not tell. And though he strove to laugh and to talk to them with greater freedom than for many a year he had used, yet his laughter rang hollow and his speech was rambling and hurried. At times when the wind from without, lulled for a moment, like a beast crouching for a spring, would suddenly leap with a roar upon the castle, shake it and pass growling in the chimney, MacLeod's strange merriment would cease as suddenly as if a plaid had been flung over his lips and he seemed as if listening,

listening intently for something which he
expected and yet dreaded to hear.

Midnight was near ; but still he refused to
leave the hall ; so they heaped the peats and
faggots on the fire and stirred it to a blaze,
waiting with him there.

What was that ? They all leaped to their
feet, their faces to the window. There, again !
Surely a shout borne on the wind ! They
listened. Again it came—someone calling for
help.

MacLeod seemed master of himself again.
His face was calm as he turned. "Go," he
cried, "see who cries yonder."

Half a dozen fled to do his bidding, leaving
him and the others standing there, watching
by the windows, peering out into the darkness ;
but nothing could be seen but the lashing of
rain and wind-tossed spray. Five minutes
passed before a young man, his garments and
hair streaming with water, rushed into the
hall, pointing behind him.

"A galley !" he cried. "A galley is being
driven on the rocks."

Perhaps the sudden call for action had
restored MacLeod ; for he seemed now less
agitated than his companions. With perfect
self-possession he gave his commands : "To
the quay," he ordered. "Get a lantern—

ropes. We'll show a light and guide them to the harbour. It is their only chance."

As some rushed to procure these means of rescue, he himself with his remaining followers, folding their plaids around them and drawing their bonnets over their brows, hurried from the hall and castle, out into the night. Against wind and rain they forced their way over the road, by rocks and tangled sea-weed to the quay and harbour in the lea of which a boat might find some shelter. The great waves rolled inwards, driven by the storm, broke and spouted upward in far-flung foam. As if a host of shrieking demons had been let loose, the gale clamoured by the cliffs, and swept inland on its turbulent way. Overhead flew the cloud-wrack, but at times, as a rent was torn in that thick and fleeting canopy, a pale glimmer of half smothered moonlight shone, revealing for a moment a tormented sea and about, a hundred yards distant in that turmoil, a tossing galley and the forms of men within her, straining for their lives at bending oars.

A few moments later, the dancing light of a lantern announced the approach of those who had been despatched to fetch it and the ropes. Reunited, the rescuing party cautiously advanced along the quay towards the opening of the little harbour adjoining. Clinging together there, their plaids fluttering about them, they stood, while MacLeod seized the lantern and, holding it aloft, swung it to and fro.

A shout from the sea told them that this signal had been seen and understood. But now came the peril to the labouring crew, of entrance by the harbour's mouth. The least error of judgment on their part and the boat must be crushed against the walls and the occupants flung to instant death. They could be seen plainly now, heaving there on the waves; one moment lost to view, the next, borne dizzily upward only to plunge again. With shouts and signals MacLeod and his party directed the galley's course—nearer, nearer until almost within leaping distance. Around the quay point it floundered. One moment of suspense as it sank in the trough of the waves and then, more by good fortune than by guidance, shot to safety.

Ready hands hauled the crew to the quay, while others lashed the boat securely. A dozen men, drenched and exhausted, had been saved and were hurried instantly to the shore. There, for a moment rescuers and rescued paused to rest and to recover breath. Utterly spent were the strangers, drooping there with bowed heads as MacLeod, still holding the lantern, advanced and held it high. " It was a very brave fight that you made against the storm," he praised; "and I bid you welcome to Dunvegan."

For a moment none answered, and then slowly one of them drew himself upright and stood calmly regarding his rescuers. And a half-smothered gasp escaped from their lips, and their hands flew instinctively to their weapons, for the man who stood before them was Donald Gorm.

For a moment all stood speechless, motionless. The eyes of his clansmen were turned on MacLeod. One word, one gesture from him and they had sprung, dirk in hand, upon those who but a moment before they had saved from death. But the chief still remained silent and gave no sign while he and his sworn enemy stood face to face.

Suddenly Donald Gorm laughed. "It is a strange chance, MacLeod," said he, "that brings us together here again and that my men and I should owe our lives to you."

"And yet I think, somehow, I knew that you would come."

"That can hardly be, since nothing was further from my mind when I set out."

"Be that as it may, Fate has decreed this meeting between us, and it shall not be said of MacLeod that even an enemy driven by storm for shelter to Dunvegan was inhospitably received."

I

" Come ! that is very handsomely said," answered Donald Gorm, laughing again, " and I shall meet you in the same spirit ; for, to tell you the truth, my men here and I are little fit for fighting."

With wondering looks MacLeod's men followed their chief, as, side by side with Donald Gorm and his followers, he escorted them to the castle.

There, presently, all was bustle and confusion. Within the hall, fuel was piled upon the fire and before it stood the men steaming in the heat. As if his guests had been his life-long friends MacLeod issued orders for their entertainment. No efforts were to be spared. Food—a feast must be set before them. The scene was quickly transformed from gloom to brightness by the glare of many lights. Torches of pine wood were fixed on spikes upon the walls, or held by attendants. Before the great open hearth an oaken board was drawn and loaded with food— pasties, venison, oaten cakes and cheese. Platters and drinking horns were placed in readiness. At the table head was drawn up the chief's chair and on either side were stools for the accommodation of those whose birth and rank entitled them to sit with him. At the lower end of the hall preparation was made for the entertainment of those of less degree.

MacLeod himself had stood directing these
arrangements, while Donald Gorm and his men
clustered by the fire. But now when all was
ready the chief turned to his guest. " Your
ghillies," he said, " can eat with my men
yonder, but do you sit here at my right hand
with my gentlemen."

" I thank you, MacLeod," answered Donald
Gorm, " but when I am away from home, like
this, with my men, I do not separate from
them, but sit with them."

" Your men will get plenty of meat and
drink without you," MacLeod urged, " so
come you with me."

" I will not take food, but with my men."

MacLeod saw that the other was not to be
moved from his resolve, so, in spite of the
black looks of his kinsmen, he ordered that all
his guests, irrespective of rank, should sit at
his own table. They gathered around, therefore, and the feast began, Donald Gorm sitting
at MacLeod's right hand.

Few words were exchanged. The rescued
men were ravenous, eagerly devouring the food
placed before them ; while around the torches
flared, casting upwards wreaths of smoke to
twine and hang in clouds about the heavy
oaken beams above them. Silently MacLeod
sat there, with set face and eyes which seemed
to look past the assembled company, as a man

might look who gazed on harrowing visions of the past. Furtively his kinsmen watched him, wondering much what dark purpose he matured, when the lightning of his vengeance would fall. Strange that he should suffer this man to eat with him! But still the chief sat there, silent.

Not so Donald Gorm; for, after a few attempts to engage his host in conversation, he abandoned the effort, and, ignoring Mac-Leod's kinsmen, turned to talk with boisterous familiarity with his own followers.

So things continued until the feast was ended and the drinking horns were filled. Again and again the audacious guest emptied his cup, and again and again it was refilled. And with every draught his face flushed a deeper crimson, a fiercer light flamed within his eyes, and his laughter rang louder. MacLeod, too, drank deeply; but instead of heating his blood the liquor seemed only to freeze him to further impassiveness.

At length becoming weary of his host's silence Donald Gorm fell to making covert and insulting references to him under cloak of conversation with his own men. "Your health, Donald! Your health, Ian!" he toasted two of their number. "I think it was silence that we wanted when the wind was screaming in our ears, and, by God, we have found it at last. It is a very good thing is silence, even in a man. Sometimes it means that he thinks the more." Here he stared meaningly at MacLeod, and added slowly; "and sometimes it means that he has an empty head."

The half smothered laughter of his men seemed to encourage him. He appeared as if possessed by reckless madness ; for suddenly leaping to his feet he held high his brimming cup. "Here's to MacLeod !" he shouted. "To the heart that knows no fear !" He waved the vessel, and whether accidentally or of set purpose, none could say, dashed the liquor so that it deluged his host's head and face.

In an instant every MacLeod, but the chief himself, was on his feet. Every hand grasped a dirk, ready to avenge the insult. For one moment it seemed that conflict must ensue; but MacLeod beckoned to his clansmen to reseat themselves. And, though still snorting and muttering their fury, they obeyed. But it was now with uneasy apprehension that they eyed him. How could he, the bravest of the brave, endure such insult ?

Never for a moment had Donald Gorm's eyes left the face of MacLeod. Still looking fixedly at him, he, too, sat down, utterly regardless of those at hand who breathed and whispered threats. Slowly his hand strayed until it had grasped the haft of his dark. Suddenly drawing his weapon he stuck it point down in the board before him and left it quivering there.

All waited, wondering what was about to follow ; but MacLeod was as if fascinated ; he leaned forward gazing at the glittering steel. Then addressing the weapon ; "was it you, was it you that killed my father?" he asked in hoarse whisper.

As if voicing his dirk Donald Gorm replied : "Aye, it has been laid to my charge that I killed a contemptible Highland laird and I do not care if I put that allegation on its second footing this night."

Silence fell, disturbed only by the panting breath of the raging men who heard this insupportable affront. They waited for their chief to strike ; but they waited in vain.

And Donald Gorm sat and glared defiance at them all. There was something so masterful in the man, so tremendous was the force of his personality, that perhaps he crushed their will in subjection to his own. They were afraid, though it may have been that their fear was less of their enemy than for the honour of their chief and clan.

"Aye," he continued, snatching the dirk from the table, "It has a point, a haft, and is sharp edged and it is held by the second best hand at thrusting it in the west."

" Whose is the other ? " asked someone.

Immediately Donald Gorm shifted the dirk from his left hand, in which he had held it, to his right. " There it is," he cried.

And not one of those who heard him dare question that braggart boast.

" And now," cried Donald Gorm arising, "let us all to bed. Right gaily, MacLeod, have you entertained us and for that we thank you ; but the hour is late and, in spite of your merriment, we are wearied men."

MacLeod too arose, and with him the others of the company ; but as if suddenly grown old, he leaned on the back of the chair and not once did he raise his eyes to the flashing eyes regarding him. His voice as he spoke was tremulous, like that of an old man. " I bid you good-night," he said, " my kinsmen will lead you to the chamber prepared for you. Your men will sleep in the kiln without."

" Not so," answered Donald Gorm. " When I am from home with my men I sleep in their very midst."

" The kiln is no fit place for you," MacLeod expostulated.

" Yet, by your leave, in the kiln will I sleep and in no other place."

" Take him there, then," MacLeod directed

his attendants, " and see that a bed is prepared for him."

Clapping his bonnet on his head, and without further word Donald Gorm strode at the head of his followers from the hall, escorted by a couple of MacLeods's attendants.

The chief watched them go, and for a few moments remained gazing, listening to their retreating footsteps. Slowly he turned and looked at his kinsmen there. They stood with bent heads. Not one would look him in the face, not one had a word to say. Slowly, as an old man, he stumbled towards the door, turned once, as if about to speak, but seemed to change his mind and passed out.

For some moments after he had gone, they too stood silent, none moved. Then suddenly, one, the youngest amongst them, smothering his face within his plaid, flung himself with head and arms resting on the table, "Ochone!" he wailed, "alas, alas, for the honour of MacLeod!" But fiercely they bade him keep silent. They would suffer no traitor thought, though shame indeed had seemed to overwhelm them. With fearful looks around they gathered by the fire, whispering. What was the meaning of it all? Impossible that he, their brave chief could fail them. Here was the moment he had prayed for—his enemy at his mercy. Some plan he must have. They must await. And so hour after hour they remained there, crouching by the fire, listening, watching, And none amongst them all ever breathed the terrible conviction that the courage of their once fearless chief had departed from his breast.

The night had almost passed. Already the eastern sky was grey, when suddenly they were aroused—stealthy footsteps, a door creaked. Next instant they sprang to their feet, for MacLeod himself stood before them. But no longer weak and vacillating; a stealthy energy seemed to animate his every movement. His eyes shone as if a flame leaped behind them. His clothing was disordered—it was evident he had not slept, "Ha, ha," he laughed, but there was something shocking in his mirth, "and so you, too, are ready. That is well. That is what I hoped for. But, hush, hush! we must not awake them." He numbered them—a dozen men. "It is enough," he said. He turned towards the table still all bestrewn with cups and platters. "It was here he sat." He pointed towards Donald Gorm's stool and suddenly kicked it violently to the floor. Drawing his dirk, as if his enemy still stood there, he stabbed and slashed the empty air, while in amazement his kinsmen stared at him. "Thus and thus I send his foul soul to hell," he gasped.

Presently he seemed to control himself with supreme effort and again he gestured for silence. '' The time has come,'' he whispered, '' Come.''

He issued his orders, and though with doubtful looks, his men followed him, as silently he led them from the hall and, at length, from the castle.

The out-house named ''the kiln'' in which the MacDonalds slept was a small thatched barn, one of which was to be found at that time, by every castle and in every township, for the preparation of corn for grinding. It had no windows, and but one means of exit by a narrow door. It was to this kiln, then, that MacLeod led his men. The violence of the storm meanwhile had subsided, and though the clouds were still driven overhead, the moon shone at intervals upon a saturated earth and tossing sea. So loudly thundered the waves that the cautious movements of the approaching party were not likely to be overheard by sleeping men. Never-the-less it was in whispers and by signs that the chief directed his followers. Without a sound they left him standing there on guard, while swiftly they sought and found a great store of faggots. These they piled before the kiln door, and around the building, silently, hardly daring to breathe, until the circle was complete. They listened—all within was still. Then they themselves, dirk in hand, surrounded the kiln ; all but three men, who, bearing torches, stood by the chief. Within the shelter of his plaid he struck a flint, lighted tinder and next moment the torches blazed. Quick as lightning they flashed about the faggots, and instantly with crackle and roar the flames lashed upward, illuminating in ruddy glare the forms of the armed men and all around, so that even the castle seemed to leap from the darkness into view. But louder than the roar of the flames was the wild yell with which MacLeod greeted the conflagration. With frightful oaths he cursed his enemy, so that even the clansmen standing there shuddered at their chief's appalling outburst and at the frenzy of his face and tossing arms. But though the flames and smoke licked and billowed about the building, no cry from within was heard. They stood around, ready to rush upon the expected fugitives from that furnace—none emerged.

Suddenly, borne upon the wind—a mocking shout somewhere from the sea. Every face was turned whence came the sound. Again, a shout of many voices ! At that moment the moon, sailing clear from clouds, shed a sickly light upon the heaving waters. They saw the black obtruding quay, the harbour wall and out from the shadow of these—a dark gliding shape.

" The galley ! The galley ! "

Their intended victims had fooled them, were even now escaping. They rushed together and almost together reached the quay ; but the boat was already beyond reach and no other was at hand. But so near were those who fled that they could be clearly seen, labouring at the oars, while in the stern sat Donald Gorm. They shouted at him insults and abuse. Turning and half rising he waved his bonnet in answer and they heard the mockery of his laughter.

Stock still in impotent, baffled fury, stood MacLeod amidst his men, watching that hated foe elude him. Then, suddenly, he screamed as might a soul in torment. Foam flecked his lips and, ere his horrified men could hold him, he had plunged into the sea. Not one amongst those whom he left behind but would, in past time, have died for him ; but now there was that in him which held them shudderingly aloof. They could but watch for him to reappear. Next moment he had arisen to the surface and they saw him madly swimming after the rapidly vanishing galley. But Donald Gorm, too, had seen that sudden plunge, and kneeling he watched the doomed man who so vainly pursued him. An order was shouted and the boat instantly ceased its forward course, heaved idly for a moment on the waves and then slowly, laboriously, was thrust backward by the oarsmen, while Donald Gorm called and beckoned to the struggling swimmer.   Nearer, nearer.

With bated breath they watched from the quay that encounter.   They saw their chief cleaving the water with great strokes, upborne, then plunged again.   They saw Donald Gorm reach out a hand as if to grasp and draw the other to safety.   Their hands met and clasped. He seemed with one arm to be upholding MacLeod.   Suddenly from the kneeling form the other hand and arm were flung upward— a glitter of steel and a dirk was buried in the swimmer's breast.   But with a choking cry the dying man grappled with the murderer, clutched at his throat, dragged him outward, and next instant, with a mighty splash, both had sunk never to reappear.

In vain the watchers on the quay waited. Sorrowfully at length they turned away. Their chief was dead; yet better perhaps that he should rest out there in peace, since there had departed from him two things without which life was not worth living.

THE BLACK RAVEN OF GLENGARRY.

Far is sàimhche an uisge,
'S ann is doimhne e.

Where the water is stillest
It is deepest.

THERE never was a chief of Glengarry to rival the Black Raven—as men called him. No, nor is there ever like to be a better. It was a brave sight when he walked down the High Street of Edinburgh, his servants in their tartans at his back, keeping the crown of the causeway and all folk turning to stare after the great Highland gentleman whom the King himself—God bless him!—delighted to honour, and with whom the Lord Justice General and other high officers of the Realm would confer on matters of the State. Aye, and it was not in Scotland only that Glengarry was held in esteem and honour; for in the Netherlands, too, was he not known as the leader whose name had become a byeword for all that was gallant in the field and sagacious in council? As for his clansmen—not one but cocked his bonnet and felt his heart beat high at a word or even a look of praise from the chief he loved. Yet, for all his well deserved reputation as a brave and successful soldier, never, during his chieftainship, did his clan know more peaceful days.

It was not so much that neighbouring chiefs feared him—though he was well calculated to inspire his enemies with fear—but rather that those whose interest it might have been to oppose him, were overborne by the weight of public opinion in his favour. Of devoted and declared allies, too, he had many, but not one more wholehearted and loyal than the chief of the very clan with which his own had, in former days, waged perpetual and relentless feud—Mackenzie of Kintail, an old man when the Raven was at the zenith of his popularity and power, but always his devoted friend. And yet that friendship had begun as surely few others ever found commencement—with Kintail flat on his back amidst the heather and the Raven kneeling on his chest, a dirk at the throat of the prostrate man.

*   *   *   *   *

But in his early days he was not known as the Raven. He was just the lad, young Ian, whom all, and not least his father, were inclined to despise. He had always, from his infancy, been unlike his two elder brothers, who were bold, adventurous, the pride of their father's heart. Ian did not excel in the chase as did they. He was the despair of old Angus, that master of the dirk and claymore, who day by day instructed the older lads in the use of these arms. Ian seemed to shrink from that violence and would rather wander solitary by moor and stream, listening to the larks singing or watching the sunbeams play on the waters. Yet, little as they heeded him, he was proud of his brothers, longed that he might win their regard, hated himself for his failure. So things had continued until the memorable day when he had seen them, armed with the fighting men of the clan, march away to battle with their inveterate enemies—the clansmen of Kintail. He was too young to accompany them. No one heeded him—the recluse. Even his father was too occupied in marshalling his followers to bid farewell to the pale-faced boy who stood with the women and the aged, staring wistfully at all that proud array. He had felt dazed, bewildered, by the shrill outcries, the barking of the dogs, the clamour of the pipes. Then he had seen his brothers, one on either side of his father, pass on, further and further until the last flutter of the tartans had been hidden from his view.

The cause of dispute with Kintail had been as of old—the boundary line of their territory, marked by the winding river that flowed between, ever changing its course as the floods

of winter hurled themselves from the snow-
covered hills, and as often, adding to the lands
of one chief that which it filched from the other.
Glengarry had at length insisted that a line,
irrespective of the river, should be drawn
between the estates ; but Kintail had scornfully rejected the proposal. High words and
insulting messages had passed between them,
until nothing remained but to settle the dispute by the sword.

So all that day the boy had waited,
sometimes climbing the hills at hand, sitting
there, watching the shadows of the clouds drift
over the shoulders of the heights—symbolic
of his own varying and alternate hopes and
fears, longing for the return of his kinsmen and
their men ; sometimes hurrying homeward
to join the little group of women who sat with
anxious eyes ever turned towards the road
by which husbands, sons, and brothers should
come again ; while others, more practical or
with less at stake, prepared the feast which
would be so sorely needed by the weary com-
batants.

The day had passed and a night of storm
and rain had fallen. He, exhausted by his
vigil, had fallen asleep by the fireside of the
castle hall, when he had been roused in panic
by a loud wailing from without—women's
voices upraised in ear-piercing accents of

K

despair and grief, and, ere he could rush out, he had been thrust back by the sudden, violent entrance of his father, followed by a dozen of his men, blood-stained, bemired, their garments in wild disarray. Without heeding him the chief had flung himself in a chair by the fireside and called for wine. Drinking deeply and then dashing the flagon to the hearth, the stricken man had then bowed his head upon his hands, while with shamed faces and in silence his followers had stood watching him and ever from without had echoed the distracted cries of the women. No words were needed to tell the boy that defeat and disaster had overtaken the clan. Followed his whispered and fearful question to one who stood near and the overwhelming tidings, in like guarded tone, that both his brothers had perished. Stunned, bewildered, unheeded, he had crept away to his bedchamber, there to sob in solitude.

Years had flown since then and he had grown to man's estate. He was still unlike others of his age, silent, taking little part in their boisterous recreations, but lithe and active. His father was now hardly over the prime of life, a vigorous man, but morose, brooding continually on the loss of his elder sons and the wrongs he had suffered at the hands of his enemy, Kintail. He was inclined to regard Ian with contempt, as an unworthy representative of their race, a son with whom he found little in common. And Ian, conscious of the disdain in which he was held, shrank from contact with his father and became more and more given to solitude.

At length an autumn came, never to be forgotten in the history of Glengarry; for the rains were torrential and, in consequence, the boundary river had overflowed its banks, inundating the adjacent pastures until all had been submerged. Never had such a flood been experienced in the memory of even the oldest inhabitants. But now the angry waters had subsided, and once again the river was found to have carved out for itself a new course, slicing from the Glengarry side long reaches of land, and proportionately adding to Kintail's possessions. Bitter were the complaints of the Glengarry herdsmen and loud the jeers of those of Kintail. Insults, and even stones had been hurled over the river. News of these encounters was not slow in reaching the ears of Glengarry himself and lashed him to frenzy. With great labour—he was no penman—he indited a letter to his enemy, renewing his insistence on a line of demarcation being drawn between the lands; and with much ceremony this missive was borne to the stronghold of Kintail. What was the rage of Glengarry when an insulting message was returned to him, bidding him learn to write, as his letter had been quite illegible. Nothing, of course, but blood, could wipe out this intolerable affront !

Again a message—verbal on this occasion—was despatched to Kintail politely inviting him and his men to meet Glengarry and his followers two days later in order that they might, once and for all, settle their difference as gentlemen should. A ready acceptance having been received, once more the fiery cross was sent far and near, summoning the clansmen, and preparations for the ensuing battle were feverishly begun. By the smithy door a group of men waited to have dirk and claymore reground, while sparks flew from the whirring, shrieking grindstone. All day long Red Hamish, the chief's piper, strode up and down rending the air with martial music, stirring his listeners with battle fever. Women, some with infants in their arms, followed wistfully after their men, well knowing that amongst these stalwart heroes must be those who would be borne back, cold and rigid, with bloodstained plaid drawn over the face that would never smile again. Dogs barked and were kicked aside ; while within the great kitchen of the castle the air was dim with smoke mingled with the steam of boiling broth, and the odour of huge joints which, in reckless prodigality, were turning on spits as preparation for the feast with which the fighting men were to be fortified for the fray on the morrow. Hither and thither strode Glengarry himself, half a dozen of his kinsmen at his back, bawling orders and directions, far too occupied with his clansmen to spare a thought for Ian, his son, who, standing moodily apart, watched this scene of activity in silent contemplation. Only, when towards dusk, the actual formation of the fighting force of some three hundred men was about to be paraded, did it occur to Glengarry that his son and heir should be present to take his rightful place. " Go, send my son to me," he bade one of his attendants.

Presently the messenger—an enormous man —returned and stood with an air of embarrassment, shuffling from one foot to the other, but without speaking a word.

" Well," demanded Glengarry, " have you told him ? "

" Aye, it was my ain sel that told her what she would be wishing her to do."

" And is he coming ? "

" No precisely coming."

" Idiot ! " snarled the chief, " what do you mean ? Speak or, by Heaven, you shall go

supperless to bed for all the fighting before
you on the morrow."

Before this awful threat the timidity of
the Highlander suddenly vanished. "She
says she'll no come," he blurted out. "Deil
a step she'll come on sic a fool's errand."

Glengarry staggered as if thunderstruck.
That he should be affronted thus before his
men! Impossible that his own son should
dishonour him. He turned a face of fury on
the gigantic ghillie who shrank, quailing like
a frightened child from the wrath of his chief.
"Dog!" he denounced, "you shall pay for
this!" And, wheeling about, he strode away
in search of Ian.

But for a time the irate father searched in
vain. Ian was nowhere to be seen. If, indeed, he had sent that message, then perhaps he
had regretted it, as well he might, and hidden
himself away. Never mind, he should be
found and an explanation forced from him.
Glengarry bawled his son's name within the
castle until the rafters rang again. No Ian
came. No other had seen him. He must
have made his escape down the glen. If need
be, bloodhounds should be set on his trail,
but meanwhile, the chief himself would pursue.
He set off madly, at every stride lashing himself to greater rage. Suddenly he became
aware that he himself was being followed, and

turning, to his speechless surprise, found himself face to face with Ian.

"I have been told that you want me," said the son, before his father could recover breath.

"What is this I hear of you?" shouted Glengarry. "What is this message you dared to send to me?"

"If you mean," answered Ian, "that you have been told of my refusal to accompany you against Kintail, you have been told truly."

For a moment Glengarry did not answer: he could not speak. Had his son struck him in the face, it had been less of a shock than to hear from his son's own lips this betrayal —as it seemed—of the honour of the clan. Somewhere in his mind the hope had been cherished that the ignorant lout who conveyed the message to him had blundered, but now, hope was swept away. "Impossible," he gasped, "impossible!"

Seeing the stricken look in his father's eyes a wave of remorse swept over the young man, and in sudden revulsion of mind his determination might in another moment have been abandoned.

"Father!" he cried, "I had no thought of paining you!" and he grasped the chief's hand.

But Glengarry flung the hand from him as if the touch were pollution. "Stand back!"

he thundered. "Coward, unworthy of the name you bear!"

"I am no coward," answered Ian hotly, again fixed in his resolve.

"What but fear could hold you back?"

"I shall tell you," Ian answered. "What is the cause of this quarrel with Kintail? It concerns the loss or gain of a few yards of land of no value. It is only pride that urges you and him to this dispute, and yet, to gratify your pride, you are willing to sacrifice precious lives. Already my two dear brothers have been lost and I, too, would, in all probability, have been killed had I been old enough at the time to be with them. For a good cause I would not hesitate to die, but for such folly I refuse."

The chief glared beneath bent brows at this son who thus defied him. "I am half minded," said he menacingly, "to strike you down with my own hand. I would to God you had died honourably, as did your brothers, rather than live to shame me as you do. But go! And may I never live to see your recreant face again." Without another word he swung about and left Ian standing with flushed and angry face.

At daybreak on the following morning the fighting men of Glengarry, led by their chief, were to set forth; but long before the dawn

Ian had donned his armour. Not a human
being stirred within the castle ; all was still
as he stole down the stair, whispering rebuke
to the watch dog as it rose with a low growl
at his approach. He unbarred the door and
in another moment stood without. Not a
light showed from the cottages at hand, where
the men slept the sleep which might be the
last from which they would awake. Stealthily
yet swiftly he made his way. Only the stars
shone overhead ; but he needed no brighter
rays : for miles around he was familiar with
every foot of the hills up which he sped. He
could hear the river roar beneath him and
night winds whispered over the heather ; but
no other sounds reached his ears. He hurried
on with all the speed he could command ; for
he was determined, if possible, to get beyond
the territory of his clan without encountering
anyone who might recognise him and carry
to his father's ears the news of his escape.
The first gray light of dawn glimmered in the
eastern sky, and he could just discern the palid
waters of Loch Loyne as he bounded down the
slopes of Glen Lyon. Though still all the
world seemed asleep, he avoided every habitation, keeping to the hillside, rather than following the tracks. Never resting, stooping, running from knoll to knoll, pausing only to re-
connoitre, then on again he ran, but the sun

had risen high ere he entered Glen Cluanie and stopped by the Loch to drink and rest his aching limbs. There he was nearly surprised by a party of men who were almost upon him before he was aware of their approach; but he lay motionless beneath the shelter of the bushes at hand and so was unobserved. He swallowed a mouthful or two of the sodden oatmeal with which he had provided himself, and then pressed onwards again.

All that day he journeyed, and only towards nightfall did he come in sight of Loch Duich by the head of which he had purposed to pass the night. He was in the Kintail country now and consequently the danger of capture was extreme. He had, therefore, to proceed with the utmost caution. There was no hope of house as shelter, or of other food than that which he had with him; so, having found a projecting slab of rock, he crept beneath it, and rolling his plaid about him, soon fell asleep.

He awakened stiff, aching in every overtaxed limb, but otherwise refreshed. Then, having consumed the last of his oatmeal, he proceeded to carry out the plan he had in mind. He knew that all the fighting men of Kintail would be mustering for the fray that day, and must either have already left their houses for this purpose, or be about to leave them. He had, therefore, only to wait for an hour or two to be

certain of safety. When he judged that that
time must have passed, he walked boldly
forth from his concealment and began to search
for what he wanted. He found it at length—
an isolated, wretched cabin, with mud-
plastered walls and dilapidated thatch. A
goat was tethered near by and a few hens
scratched about the door. Still keeping himself out of sight, he sat down to watch.
Presently, out from the cottage door sped a
child, almost naked, and, with shrill cries of
glee, went scampering down a path. Next
instant a comely young woman, presumably
the mother, rather dishevelled, thrust her
head out and seeing her escaping infant,
immediately gave chase, captured it, delivered some hearty smacks and then bore the
now howling culprit home.

Still Ian waited ; but as no one else emerged
from the house, he arose presently and
cautiously approached. He peeped in through
the doorway. The mother was engaged in
dressing the child, no other than these was
there, her back was turned. She had neither
seen nor heard the onlooker. Ian knocked.
The woman turned, staring for a moment
speechlessly, and then, seeing before her an
armed man, wearing the red badge of Glengarry, she threw her arms around the child and
started up with a shriek.

"You need have no fear," Ian reassured her. "I will do you no harm."

"What is it you want here?" asked the woman, backing into a corner as she spoke.

"I shall tell you," replied Ian, "but first you must answer my question; where is your husband?"

"He has gone to the fighting. Woe is me that I should have to say so, and weary is the day that leaves me here alone with my bairn to face a MacDonell of Glengarry."

"Yes," said Ian, "I am a MacDonell of Glengarry; but, unlike others of my name, I have come here to make peace, not war."

"Oh Sir! What do you mean?"

"Listen," Ian continued, "I have refused to take part with the men of my clan in this fight and have come here only that I may, if possible, avert it. Your husband is with your clan which will be opposed to mine. Help me, and, if my attempt should succeed, your husband will return to you this day in honour, without a blow having been struck."

"And how can I help you?"

"Lend me a plaid of the MacKenzie tartan."

"I have my husband's bonny new plaid to be sure; but what would you be wanting with that?"

"I must disguise myself before I can approach your chief; otherwise I should be

shot down before ever I could draw near, and
near him I must be if I am to have the speech
with him that I desire."

"And will you return it ? "

"I promise, and here is my own ," said he,
handing his plaid to her.   "Keep it until I
return the other."

The woman hesitated, eyeing Ian ; but,
reassured by the honesty of his look, she at
length handed over to him her husband's
plaid, and stood in her doorway watching him
as, with the MacKenzie tartan wrapped around
him, he hurried from her dwelling.

He had not proceeded far by the side of the
loch before he encountered fighting men of the
MacKenzie clan, sometimes singly, at others,
in groups of two or three, hurrying to their
place of assembly on Donan Isle.   They hailed
him, inviting him to accompany them ; but he
excused himself on one pretext or another, and
so succeeded in continuing his journey alone.
When, however, he reached the point from which
he must cross the intervening water in order
to reach the island, he found a considerable
concourse of clansmen gathered together, and
with these he mingled freely, without exciting
the least surprise.   They were waiting their
turn to be rowed across to the island, and, in
due course, Ian himself was thus conveyed.

On the island a scene of great activity met his gaze. Already nearly three hundred men, arrayed for battle, had collected, some sitting in moody silence apart, others talking and jesting together. To and fro strutted a piper, his tartan waving, as his pipes screamed forth the gathering pibroch of the clan. On a level stretch of sward long tables had been placed, laden with food—bannocks, oatcakes, joints of mutton and venison from the hills, interspersed with great flagons of ale. The hungry Highlanders eyed this abundance impatiently, ready to spring to the attack ; but none dare seat himself or touch a morsel until Kintail should give the signal. The chief with his leading men and close kinsmen was conferring apart, beneath the shelter of some overhanging trees. Ian, sitting alert and vigilant, had observed him there, and never for an instant had he ceased to keep watch upon him. Presently the conference seemed to end, for Kintail turned abruptly, and, with his kinsmen straggling behind, he strode in amongst his men. He, like Glengarry, was of middle age ; but of less robust build than the other, and his features marked him as one of a certain refinement and nobility of mind as of race. He greeted many of his followers by name as he passed, pausing at times to exchange a few words with others, always with perfect freedom and a kindly cordiality, which endeared him to their hearts. On such occasions great familiarity was permitted and little ceremony observed—a family gathering at which the chief was accessible to all. At length he seated himself at the head of the central table and signalled to the expectant clansmen to occupy the rough benches placed in readiness for them. Immediately a general rush ensued, men pushed their way forward, eager for accommodation at the board, irrespective of rank—such was the freedom sanctioned. Ian, however, experienced some difficulty in placing himself in close proximity to the chief, but succeeded so far that only one man intervened between them.

With his plaid wrapped around him, he turned towards his companion and touched his sleeve. "I have a favour to ask," said he.

The youth—he was a young cousin of the chief—stared at Ian in some surprise. "What is that?" he asked.

"There is a private matter of urgency that I wish to communicate to Kintail," whispered Ian. "I should deem it a favour if you would exchange places with me."

The young man hesitated, but impressed by the authority in Ian's tone—obviously that of one of gentle birth—he bowed politely and rising, surrendered his place as requested.

Ian thanked him warmly and cast a stealthy glance around. Not one save himself was unoccupied. Each man present had drawn his dirk and stuck it, point down, in the board before him, and with teeth and fingers was busy with the plentiful food.

The chief himself was thus engaged ; but he paused to glance at the stranger by his side. "You do not eat, friend," he remarked.

"Before I eat," answered Ian, "there is something I must say to you."

Kintail stared at him. "First, tell me who you are ; " said he ; "for I do not seem to know your face."

Ian again looked swiftly down the table ; none observed him. He arose, and bending, whispered in Kintail's ear : "My name is Ian MacDonell of Glengarry."

Kintail bounded to his feet. "What ? " he cried.

Instantly Ian threw off the plaid which had enveloped him, disclosing the red badge of his clan, sprang like a deer-hound on the chief, locked his arms around him and flung him to the earth ; then, kneeling on him there, held a dirk with its point pressing on the throat of the prostrate man.

Kintail lay helpless ; but not so his clansmen. After one moment of astounded silence, with a roar of rage they arose, snatching their dirks, tumbling over the forms, the tables, and themselves in frantic wrath.

But ere one could rush to the rescue, with a shout that drowned their outcries, Ian arrested them. "Stand back," he yelled; "or your chief dies."

For a second they paused uncertain; the next it seemed that a hundred dirks must be plunged in the body of the madman who defied them; but Ian held them. "Move but hand or foot," he cried, "and I thrust my dirk home. See! Its point is on his throat and if I fall he, too, will never rise again. I do not seek his death, or the death of any one of you. I come only to stop the madness of this warfare with my clan. With an unsettled boundary line between our lands there can be no settled peace. I ask you, Kintail, now to agree to this dividing line; for if you will not, then, by Heaven, you shall die."

Not a man of all the raging Highlanders dared stir; they saw the look of iron resolution in Ian's eyes and knew that their chief's life was at stake. They stood silent. Only he could answer.

"If you will swear to agree to this division," continued Ian, addressing the chief, "then I shall throw my dirk aside and you may do with me as you will."

Kintail gazed on the set, determined face

L

bent above him. "I surrender to your gallantry," said he, "rather than to your threat."

"Swear," Ian bade.

Kintail advanced his head and kissed the dirk at his throat. "On the cold steel of your dirk," he declared, "I swear agreement with your terms."

Ian sprang to his feet and, hurling his dirk on the ground, stepped aside.

But Kintail, too, arose, and picking up the discarded weapon, handed it back to Ian. "A gallant gentleman," said he, "shall always be honoured in Kintail."

The chivalrous magnanimity of their chief was, to his emotional Highlanders, as fire to tow. They shouted. They threw their bonnets in the air. They pressed around him; but he waved them back. "We waste time," he cried. "Let us not neglect the good cheer, the less so that we have now a guest of honour!"

And so it was that, once more with Ian at Kintail's right hand, the repast was continued.

Half an hour later the clan of Kintail, headed by the chief with Ian by his side, marched to the place appointed for battle with Glengarry. Perhaps in the heart of the younger and more ardent of these fierce tribes-

men, a lingering regret may have lurked that
the bonny fight for which they had been
summoned was now little likely to take place;
but, if such disappointment there were, it was
suppressed in loyalty to their chief's decision.
Not a trace of ill-will was manifested towards
Ian, hereditary foe though he was—his
gallantry had commended him to those who
valued honour and courage more than life
itself. On the whole, therefore, the throng
that marched was light-hearted and gay—
pipes skirling, tartans waving, song and
laughter enlivening the way.

Very different was the demeanour of the
Glengarry clan when, the shoulder of the hill
having been passed, that grim array first came
in sight. By the Bridge of Shiel they had
planned to encounter, and on the farther side
of the river Ian could see the men of his clan
drawn up in battle order. They plainly
purposed to dispute the passage of the bridge.
He could recognise his father in the forefront,
his kinsmen at his side. There they stood,
silent, menacing; but a wild yell of defiance
arose as they sighted the head of the advancing
column, and recognised the tartans of Kintail.

But, while some hundred of yards separated
the opposing forces, Kintail gave order to his
men to halt and he, himself, with Ian and a
ghillie bearing a flag of truce, advanced to

meet Glengarry until about fifty paces from the bridge and there they, too, paused.

Suddenly from the Glengarry clansmen a murmur arose, swelling to clamour—they had in amazement and dismay recognised Ian with their foes, and supposed that he was held prisoner to ransom. Glengarry himself rushed across the bridge and immediately his men would have followed tumultuously after him; but turning with upraised claymore, he shouted to them, bidding them stand where they were; then alone, with burning eyes, he strode towards Ian and his companion. Ignoring Kintail, he glared at his son.

"How comes it," he demanded furiously, "that I find you with our enemies?"

"They are no enemies of mine," answered Ian.

Shame unimagined, shame worse than death seemed to the wretched Glengarry to have overwhelmed him! What could this mean but that his son, his only remaining son, had betrayed their honour, had gone over to the enemy? There was but one way in which this stain could be washed out. "Traitor!" he cried, "Unfit to live," and he swept aloft his sword to smite Ian to the earth.

But Kintail was too quick for him. He caught the upraised wrist and with one wrench tore the claymore from Glengarry's hand and threw it on the ground. "Are you mad?" he cried. "Would you kill the man who, single-handed, has won the victory for you this day?"

Glengarry stared, speechless and panting.

"Never was braver deed than that done by your son," Kintail continued, and he told him of Ian's exploit. "He has achieved more it may be," he concluded, "than you with all your clan at your back, could ever have done; for to him I have promised to agree to a permanent division of our lands."

Slowly Glengarry turned a face of tragic remorse towards his son. "Ian," he stammered. "Ian . . .," and could say no more.

But Ian, laughing, grasped his father's hand and wrung it. "All is well, Father," he answered, "yet there lacks one thing. Since Kintail can find in his generous heart forgiveness for the ill-mannered coup I gave him, it is we who are forever in his debt. Here and now, therefore, let us pledge our friendship." And he held his father's readily surrendered hand towards the extended hand of Kintail.

So the two chiefs pledged a friendship destined never to be broken. But one last tribute Kintail paid to Ian before they parted. Dropping Glengarry's hand, he seized that of Ian and leading him forward faced the MacDonell clansmen.

"Happy are you," he cried, "to have a young chief such as he; a braver you can never have. On the merciful errand of the white dove of peace, he, the black raven of war, has winged his way this day."

And they caught up the name : "The Black Raven!" they shouted. "The Black Raven!" and so, as the Black Raven he was known until his death.

MACEUAR.

Theid seòltachd thar spionnadh.

Cunning overcomes strength.

WHEN the gray sea mists of the Atlantic hang over the distant Hebridean isle of Tiree and the long ocean swell breaks in thunder on the beach, majestically, above the smothering clouds and oblivious to all unrest, the giant shoulders of the hill Beinn Hynish tower to the sunlight.

In spring you may wander on its eastern side and find gentle slopes with grassy banks where primroses and wild hyacinths bloom. Flocks of golden plover soar about you, larks fill the air with their music, and heather moths flit lazily on the breeze. But woe betide the benighted wanderer; for seaward, great cliffs fall sheer to the ocean beneath, and from these rugged steeps the peregrine falcon and raven wheel and sea-gulls clamour. Looking thence you may note a long spur of rock which projects into the sea, and around which strong currents race and foam.

* * * * * *

Generations have come and gone; but mountain and glen and coast remain unchanged. The inhabitants of past centuries looked on scenes unaltered to the eyes of the traveller of to-day.

It was beneath the shadow of Beinn Hynish that in long distant days there lived a youth named Euar MacEuar. Left an orphan in infancy he had been adopted by his foster-mother and by her had been brought up with the utmost devotion. He was the last of an ancient name, and, as he grew, his grace of bearing and fearless spirit bore evidence to his descent. From his earliest years he found a friend and constant companion in one of his own age, Black Alan, so named from his swarthy complexion. In all manly exercise these boys excelled. Together they would climb the cliffs where none other than they dared set foot ; nimble as the deer, they could leap over chasms from which the boldest without shame might have shrunk; and like the seal they could swim without fatigue. In one particular only had Euar the advantage : he was by far the better archer. So skilful did he become in the use of his weapon that, even before reaching his full strength, he could draw to his ear a bow with which others could barely reach to the breast. He could loose his shafts with such rapidity that three were simultaneously in the air ; and his range extended a full fifty paces farther than that of any other marksman. His dexterity, however, was limited in this respect : it depended on his use of one bow ; with none other than his own was he superior in archery to his friend.

He was a fanciful youth and gradually he seemed to regard his weapon as if itself were animate. He would whisper to it, imploring it to be true, before loosing his shaft. He would caress and fondle it when the mark was hit, as usually was the case. Resting it on his knees as he sat by the fire on winter nights he would sing to it, as might a lover to his mistress, songs of praise. Day by day and all day long it was in his hand, and by night it stood by his bedside. It was his most treasured possession. Now, Alan, though careful to conceal his feelings on this score, had always cherished a bitter jealousy that he should be thus surpassed in skill ; and therefore, when one day Euar's bow was missing, his foster-mother, who had mistrusted Alan from the first, suspected him of having stolen it. But when questioned he stoutly denied all knowledge of the weapon's whereabouts, nor could Euar be persuaded to doubt his friend's innocence in the matter.

The woman, however, had the courage of her convictions, and did not scruple to accuse Alan to his face. " Aye," she railed at him, " black is your hair and black the heart that prompted you to steal from the friend that trusted you ;

but, if the bow be not returned, the day shall come when you shall rue your ill-gotten possession."

With scowling countenance Alan turned in silence from her and strode away ; but Euar, ever generous of heart, pursued him and would not suffer their friendship thus to be severed. Nevertheless from that day there were times when Alan looked at him askance and never seemed wholly to have forgotten the accusation brought against him by the woman, nor her ominous malediction.

In spite of all, however, the friendship continued, and the lads were constantly together, though never again would Alan enter his companion's house.

"He will bring bad luck to you," Euar's foster-mother would often warn him.

But he paid no heed to her prognostications.

So things continued until both youths had reached their twenty-first year. Both were remarkably handsome, tall and active. Maidens were not lacking on the island who stole admiring glances at the young men who, nevertheless, seemed singularly proof against all feminine allurements, until one memorable evening at length came to alter the even tenor of their lives.

An angry sun had sunk beneath the far horizon of the ocean, and a strong westerly

gale blowing up had overcast a lowering sky
and lashed the sea to giant breakers which
rolled thunderously on the rocky shore. The
coming night seemed likely to be one of tempest. All day the two friends had been together in the hills and had parted not far from
Euar's house, Alan making his way homeward
across the intervening shoulder of the mountain.

Euar had found his foster-mother awaiting
him, sitting by the fire, and busily knitting
a pair of hose intended for his wear. He had
been impatient for his supper which she had
prepared ; but, before devouring it, was first
urged to try on one of these coverings for the
legs, a procedure rendered difficult by the
presence of needles still protruding from the
handiwork. An argument had ensued ; which
had led to the young man's good-natured
laughter and submission, so ending an incident,
trifling at the moment, but destined to prove
long after a determining factor in his destiny.

Hardly had he commenced his meal thus
delayed when to his surprise he heard Alan's
voice from without shouting his name. He
knew that for no trifling reason would his
friend, who was detested by his foster-mother,
approach so closely to her presence. Convinced, therefore, that he was urgently needed,
and deaf to the protests of the dame who in

vain sought to detain him, he crammed his bonnet on his head and rushed from the house.

Alan was awaiting him close at hand. " A boat," he cried, " a boat out yonder, caught in the currents and like to be dashed on the rocks."

Without further parley they ran towards the shore and soon came in view of the tumbling waves and spouting foam, the rocky coast and headland, and close to these, heaving on the angry storm-tossed sea, the small open boat which Alan had seen from the hill track far above. Already a little band of men and women had gathered on the beach, their garments fluttering in the wind, gazing out anxiously towards the endangered boat and its occupants. These were apparently two in number—an old man and a maid and both laboured desperately at the oars. One of the spectators, an experienced fisherman, had advanced as closely as he dared to the seething breakers, and by shouts and signals sought to direct the boat's course ; but whether in that turmoil his voice was lost and his gesticulations unobserved, or whether the frail crew were unable to obey him, was uncertain.

In either case the boat continued to be swept near and ever nearer to imminent destruction. One chance only of safety remained—if it could be brought under the lea of the long

projecting spur of rock which afforded a certain amount of protection from the violence of
the gale ; but even there the danger from
half-submerged rocks was very great.   From
that standpoint, however, a rescue might
just possibly be effected were the boat to be
wrecked.   To the two young men the thought
flashed simultaneously, and together they
raced for the rock.   Together they reached it,
and on hands and knees, deluged and half-
blinded with spray, slipping perilously over
tangle and seaweed, inch by inch they
advanced until the boat was a bare stone's
cast from them.   They shouted directions
and their voices seemed to be heard, for, as if
in answer, the girl's face turned for a second
towards them, and a less dangerous course was
set.   Like the fangs of a hungry monster
eager to devour its prey, the jagged points
of rock were thrust upward, while around them
the waters burst in foam, but one after another
was passed in safety.   A little nearer, only a
little nearer, and then these two could surely
be dragged from death.   On the crest of a great
wave they came.   Euar saw the danger—the
black menace of rock for a moment showing
from the water.   He shouted in vain.   Crash !
They had struck.   The shattered boat was
instantly swamped and the old man flung into
the sea from which his body was never to be

recovered. The girl sprang upright and for a moment, ere the boards beneath her sank, she stood, her long dark hair blowing upon the wind, her arms outheld. She shrieked in horror, once, and then she, too, was plunged into the waves. For a second the two young men stared in horror at the spot where she had sunk. Then, they saw her reappear, again borne inwards by the surge, only a few yards from them.

"Stay!" Euar shouted to his companion, and, without a moment's delay, leaped into the sea. He sank, but when he rose again he was holding the girl in his arms. Fortune favoured them for the next wave bore them within Alan's reach. With one hand holding to the rock, the other outstretched, he strained towards them, grasped the girl's hand and drew them in together. Clasping her, he lifted her bodily from the water, leaving Euar to fend for himself. The half-submerged man would assuredly have been torn away and engulfed by the following breaker, but the girl still desperately clutched him, nor could Alan disengage her hold until all three were lying prostrate and gasping on land. Soon others came hastening to their aid, and by these the girl was conveyed to safety.

This young maiden's widowed mother had died in the adjacent island of Coll, and the daughter had determined to seek out relatives in Tiree and throw herself on their hospitality. To the house of these kinsfolk, Ailsa (such was her name) was therefore borne, and by them was kindly received, and soon by the sweetness and charm of her disposition, no less than by her beauty, she had won the hearts of all with whom she came in contact.

But none was more completely captivated by her than the two young men to whom she owed her life. Sometimes together, at others singly, they sought her company, and for long none could tell which of the two found greater favour in her eyes. Indeed, she could not, at first, herself have chosen between them : with either she seemed to be content. While Euar appealed to her gayer and more tender emotions, she was none the less fascinated by the bold and masterful Alan.

For the first time in the friendship of these two companions a breach seemed inevitable : both were in love with the same girl, and neither concealed his passion, though for long neither referred directly to the subject. Each was keenly alive to the momentous decision which must sooner or later be reached and which must desolate the life of one. It was Alan who at length broke the reserve between them.

The two men were walking together from

Ailsa's house one evening. They were silent, each occupied with his own rather moody reflections. Alan suddenly stopped dead, facing his companion. "I have had enough of this," he declared.

"What do you mean by that, Alan?" asked Euar in surprise.

"I think you know very well what I mean. Why should we pretend friendship when we both would give the world to be quit of the other at the present time? I love her and mean to win her in spite of our friendship."

Euar regarded the flashing eyes of his companion. "There you are wrong," he answered calmly; "for I think I am the one she loves."

"You lie," shouted Alan, and clapped his hand on his dirk.

In another instant it seemed that they must have fallen to blows, but with an effort Euar controlled his anger. "Stay," he bade, and, though his opponent now held his drawn weapon in his hand, he continued: "For the love that I have borne you, Alan, I would be loath to fight with you. It is for her to say which of us she will have. Let us make an agreement. To-morrow both of us shall ask her as wife, and which shall ask first we shall decide by drawing lots. Let us swear that whoever is rejected will bear no malice, but continue still the friend that he has ever been."

To these proposals Alan sullenly agreed and both, on the bare steel of their dirks, pledged themselves to fidelity. It was Alan who subsequently held the straws of unequal length, and in his grasp remained the longer which gave him priority of opportunity with Ailsa. With a shout of exultation he greeted his good fortune, and having announced his intention of visiting the girl the following morning, he bade Euar good-night and departed.

But early next day it chanced that Ailsa was much occupied with household duties and so, though Alan was at her door betimes, the hour was late before she was prepared to accompany him alone, as he urged her to do. At length noon, indeed, had passed ere she announced her readiness, and together they set forth to the hillside where he had determined to make known to her his love. Hardly, however, were they seated when, to his fury, he saw Euar approaching. With an oath he leaped to his feet again and bade the other begone.

" Why should I go ? " demanded Euar. " You have had the morning together which was what we agreed to. I think I have more right here now than you."

" That is a question which can be settled

M

but in one way," cried Alan, and, dirk in hand, he rushed upon his rival.

But Ailsa was in no mind to have her choice of lovers thus settled for her. She flew upon Alan and with unexpected dexterity wrenched the weapon from his hand. "Who are you," she cried, "to decide which of my friends shall visit me and which may not? Think shame of yourself that you should attack a man who has never said an ill word of you, though many you have spoken of him."

Alan glared at her. "Give me back my dirk," he demanded.

"Not until you promise that you will not fight."

"You would protect him," he sneered.

"Rather I protect you, who cannot keep your dirk even from a woman."

"You love him," he accused.

"That is no concern of yours."

"Take him, then," he shouted, "and may you both go to Hell.

She laughed and threw his dirk after him as he rushed away; but she burst into tears as Euar took her in his arms, and though at first she attempted to thrust him from her, and protested that she hated both him and his rival, yet presently she seemed to find comfort in his embrace and no longer resisted it. After a time, however, she withdrew from him and they sat together on a bank. He spoke gaily to her and soon dispelled her gloom, making her smile again. For an hour they sat thus until it was time for her to go. He had spoken no word of love, but, as she would have arisen, he detained her, and drawing a chain of gold from his pocket hung it around her neck.

"You take me captive?" she laughed.

"Will you find the bondage dull?" he asked.

"No." She toyed with the trinket. "Its symbol is of gold."

"And enduring?" he questioned.

"Enduring enough to hang endlessly next my heart."

He captured her hand. "Have you aught to give ME, Ailsa?" he asked.

"A mercenary," she accused, "who cannot give but only barter."

"On the contrary," he corrected—"a bankrupt who has given his all."

She took a ring from her finger and slipped it on one of his. "Will that recompense you?" she asked. "You see my gift, too, is one of gold."

"And a symbol?" he whispered.

"It is a symbol."

"Ailsa!" he cried, and clasped her in his arms.

Thus it was that Ailsa and Euar plighted their troth.

It was much to the credit of Alan that when the betrothal was announced to him he showed no ill-will to the lovers. If jealousy rankled in his heart, the emotion was suppressed. To the surprise and delight of Euar he greeted him without a trace of his former spleen. Only towards Ailsa did his demeanour undergo change ; he was distantly polite when they met ; and he took care that these meetings should be rare.

For her part, though she truly loved Euar, it was evident that she had not quite dismissed from her mind his former rival, would often cast rather wistful glances after his retreating form, and was inclined to hint that jealousy on Euar's part was the cause of Alan's avoidance of her. " Can we not still be friends ? " she asked of him one day.

" What need have you of my friendship ? "

" One never knows," she smilingly retorted. " I should like to count you always as my friend."

He looked steadfastly at her for a moment. " If you should ever need my friendship," he told her, " it shall be yours until I die."

Weeks passed happily for the two lovers, and even Alan seemed reconciled to his fate. The friendship for which Ailsa had asked, he

seemed prepared to give, neither expecting nor
desiring more.   Naturally he spent less time
in Euar's company than formerly, and was
often to be seen prowling about the hills alone,
or in his boat, in which, sailing about the coast
or even far out to sea, he would be absent for
hours.   He became silent and morose, and
seemed disinclined for any companionship,
brooding on his sorrow.

There were many on the island, who, knowing of his disappointment and marking his
solitude, were full of sympathy for him, but
none more so than the lovers.   Euar was
distressed that his own good fortune should
have been the cause of his friend's misery, the
more so that Alan had accepted with such
apparent generosity the turn of fate in his dis-
favour ;   while Ailsa could not fail to be
touched by a devotion which she could never
requite. They often spoke of him, trying to
devise means for his diversion, and in this
respect Ailsa was very urgent, willing even,
to be left alone at times in order that Euar
might bear his friend company.

Euar's foster mother was of a different
mind : she was glad that Alan should no longer
be on such close terms of intimacy with her
foster-son as had formerly been the case.   Her
opinions were, however, rather at a discount,

for her reception of Ailsa as his future bride had not been enthusiastic.

One morning Euar was early astir, and was busying himself with clubs and other weapons, when his foster-mother confronted him in alarm at these warlike preparations. "What need have you of these?" she asked.

He laughed at the anxiety of her looks. "I go to make war only with seals," he answered her.

"Does Ailsa accompany you?" she asked.

"No, for she has bidden me go rather with Alan, and so with Alan alone I go."

The woman approached him and laid her hand caressingly on his head as he knelt beside her. "Ah, Euar," she pleaded, "you are dear to me as if indeed you were my son. If you love me, do not go with Alan to-day."

"Mother," he answered "for you are the only mother I have ever known. I would gladly obey you had you reasons for delaying me; but well I know that you have none."

"Listen to me," she pleaded. "If you go with Alan this day evil will befall you. All night long strange voices have called from the sea. Twice I heard a raven croak at daybreak! These are omens sent to warn you, and black is the shadow of fear that hangs over my heart. Do not go, I beseech you."

But he only laughed at her superstitions,

and, having completed his preparations for the chase, bade his foster-mother farewell and hurried away.

Alan met him on the shore and together they launched their boat, pushed out to sea and were already hoisting their sail when Euar's foster-mother came hurrying down the beach.

With forebodings of disaster still oppressing her, she had determined to make one last appeal for the abandonment of the expedition, and now stood, her grey hair streaming in the wind, beckoning and calling. But her efforts were in vain; for though Alan saw her and guessed her purpose, he paid no heed, nor drew Euar's attention to her, while he, sitting with back turned towards the shore, was quite unaware of her presence there.

The woman waited, watching until the boat had rounded the headland; then, suddenly realising that by calling after the voyagers, as she had done, she had inadvertently added yet another to the omens of misfortune, she turned and retreated, muttering, to her house again, There she occupied herself with domestic duties for the remainder of the morning, and at length sat by her fire, spinning. She was thus employed when she heard Euar's dog barking furiously and, a moment or two later, a tap at the door. She arose wondering who her visitor might be and, throwing open the door, was surprised to see Ailsa standing before her. As before said, she had never shown much cordiality towards the girl, who, sensible of the older woman's half-veiled dislike, had seldom entered the house. Nothing, however, had been said by either regarding this hostility and to outward appearance the two were on friendly footing. It was therefore with apparent goodwill that Ailsa was welcomed on this occasion and bidden to enter : " Aye, and is that you, Ailsa ? It is lonely that you will be this day wanting the two lads who have left you behind."

" I wish Euar were back," Ailsa answered as she entered and sat by the fire on the stool offered to her. " When will he return ? "

" Indeed I think you should know more about that than I, for it was to please you that he went."

" And if it were so," Ailsa retorted, " it was only that I do not wish Euar's love for me to separate him from his friend." The older woman eyed her grimly. " I cannot deny that you have won my boy's love," she said, " See that you keep it as a sacred thing."

" I love him with all my heart," cried the girl, " and am wretched awaiting his return."

" Why did you send him, then, with black Alan ? " fiercely demanded the angry woman.

"Answer me that, you that tell me you love him ! "

"What do you mean ? " asked Ailsa in astonishment.

"What do I mean ? " her accuser repeated. "I mean that he has gone on an ill-omened errand. I mean that if you love him as you say you do, you may rue the day you sent him with that black-hearted man."

"You think he is in danger ? " cried Ailsa, starting to her feet.

But the foster-mother turned aside. "How should I know what danger threatens him ? " she answered sourly.

"Let us go and watch for them," pleaded Ailsa.

"Aye, let us go and watch for them."

Together they sat on the beach, wrapped in plaids against the chill wind, and waited for the return of the boat. Little was said between them as they watched the gulls sweep and soar above the waters, and the rollers break about the rocks in long-drawn sighs. Dull and gray stretched the wide expanse of ocean before them—the sullen mystery of the sea. An hour passed—two hours.

Ailsa was bitterly cold and wearied by this monotonous vigil, she was hungry too, and would gladly have returned ; yet, somehow, she felt ashamed of her impatience and for some time she hesitated to express her longing. At length, however, feeling no longer able to support her misery, she turned to her companion. "Why should we wait here, perishing of cold?" she asked.

"You are no colder than Euar is like to be—out there drenched by the sea."

"But we cannot hasten his return by ourselves freezing in this icy wind."

"Let your love for him warm you," the grim woman answered as she sat unmoved, her elbows resting on her knees, her chin upon her hands, gazing out to sea. She seemed herself impervious to the rigours of the weather.

Ailsa looked askance at her, and suddenly felt something like panic agitating her breast. At all costs she must escape from this terrifying companion. She sprang to her feet. "Wait for him if you will," she cried, "but I shall go."

But the older woman caught her wrist and dragged her down again. Without loosing her grip, "You shall stay," she declared, and turned on the girl a set face in which the eyes glittered like steel, "you must learn hardihood if you would be the bride of MacEuar."

Quite unable to resist the hold which was not for an instant relaxed from her wrist, trembling betwixt cold and fear, Ailsa resigned herself to her fate. Tears welled from her

eyes ; but she fought them back. She would
not add to the triumph of the other by display
of such weakness.   She crouched there shiver-
ing and silent.

How long they continued to sit Ailsa could
not tell. She remained with closed eyes,
oblivious of time. Suddenly her companion
bounded to her feet, pulling her, too, upright.
Half dazed Ailsa stared at her and saw her
pointing a long, lean arm and hand outward
toward the sea.

"See ! " cried the foster-mother. "See
there ! "

Ailsa looked and saw far out to sea a boat
approaching. It rose and fell on the waves,
its sail leaning to the wind, but whether it was
the boat they waited for or not, she could not
tell. But the foster-mother was in no doubt.
" It is his boat," she declared.

" I shall tell Euar of your unkindness to me,"
sobbed Ailsa.

But the other paid no heed to the threat.
She stood shading her eyes with her hand,
gazing towards the approaching boat. Ten
minutes passed. They could see now the spray
dashed from the bow of the tossing craft.
Next moment the older woman uttered a
piercing scream, " There is but one man in it ! "
and, dragging Ailsa with her, fled towards
the promontory by the lea of which the boat

would shelter. And then, as panting they paused, " It is Black Alan," she wailed, " my Boy ! my Boy ! "

Trembling, with dread in her heart, Ailsa looked. It was as the other had said : Alan alone occupied the boat. But still, perhaps their fears were needless : he had landed Euar somewhere on the coast and so was returning without him. All must be well ; surely all must be well.

Not another word spoke the foster-mother. She stood immovable as the rock beneath her, staring with a terrible look in her eyes towards the solitary boatman as he lowered the sail and ran the boat to land. She still stood motionless as he fumbled with the gear ; but when he stood upright and leaped ashore, she seemed to shake off the sort of frozen rigidity in which she had been held. Casting aside the girl who clung to her, she rushed upon Alan, clutching him, " Where is my boy ? " she shrilled. " Where is my boy ? "

Alan stood dripping with sea water. Water streamed from his hair. His downcast face was haggard and pale like that of one arisen from long sickness. He did not return her gaze and he choked as he struggled for utterance. " It was not my fault," he stammered.

" What was not your fault ? Speak ! Tell me, where is Euar ? " she demanded.

" I was standing too far from him to help when he fell from a cliff into the sea."

" But he can swim."

" He must have struck his head on a rock, for he sank like a stone and never rose again."

" He is drowned," she wailed.

Suddenly he violently flung off her hold of him. " Do you think I would not have saved him if I could? I swam to where he had sunk. I dived again and again. Only when no more strength remained to me did I despair."

A piercing cry rang from Ailsa's lips interrupting him, and he turned to see her, sunk upon the rock, her face hidden in her hands. He would have sprung towards her ; but the older woman seized his arm and perforce confronted him again.

" God knows whether or not your story be true," she cried, " but if you have used treachery towards my foster-son, then may God's curse rest on you and yours."

He eyed her darkly. " Do you dare accuse me ? " he asked.

" I have known you ever to be false," she denounced.

They stood face to face and his eyes were the first to shift. With a muttered oath he turned aside.

" And as for you," she continued, turning towards the prostrate girl. " Here is the man whose friendship you have bought with Euar's life—take him, and may I see you no more!" She flung her plaid about her and bending her head fled from them both.

For some moments Alan stood hesitating; then, seeming to summon resolution, he advanced and stooping, very gently touched Ailsa's shoulder. "I would gladly have died to save him," he whispered. "You will believe that of me, will you not?"

She raised her tear-stained face, regarding him. "Yes," she said, "I believe you, Alan."

It was with the utmost tenderness that he raised her and conveyed her to her home.

The courting of Ailsa by Alan followed from that day; though at first and indeed for many a week he was too circumspect to attempt to see her; but he took care that she should have occasions to keep him in kindly remembrance. He contrived to render her certain services; little gifts were sent by him; though he himself held aloof. And when at length they met it was of Euar's death and his own sense of bereavement in the loss of his life-long friend that he spoke with much pathos. As time passed, however, their meetings were more frequent and longer, until it became evident to all that he intended, if he could, to occupy the place which Euar had held in her affections. For her part, though she truly mourned the

man to whom she had been betrothed, the force
of Alan's personality seemed to overpower her ;
she seemed less and less able to withstand his
wooing.

One summer morning she was waiting for
Alan at a spot near the shore, where he had
persuaded her that she should meet him.   Her
mind had been in a turmoil—she had hardly
slept the previous night ; for Alan, at their
last meeting had been insistent, demanding
her decision regarding him, and she had
promised to give a definite answer.   She would
marry him, that she had determined, and yet,
somewhere within her heart a voice called still
for the lover she had lost.

"You that my son loves."   Suddenly someone spoke from behind her.

Ailsa leaped to her feet to find Euar's foster-
mother standing grim and forbidding but a few
feet from her.   They had met since the day
of Euar's loss ; but no word had passed between them.   Ailsa stood speechless.

"You wait for your lover," the older woman
continued.

"That is no concern of yours," the girl
retorted.

"That is a true word you have spoken ;
what you do is of no concern to me ; yet
Euar loves you and on his account I have come
to warn you."

" Of what would you warn me ? "

" Lest you betray his love."

" You are cruel," cried Ailsa, stifling her rising sobs. " Euar is dead, and though I shall never forget him, I am young and have my life to live. Why should I not live it with the man whom he, too, loved ? "

" Euar is not dead."

For some moments Ailsa stood motionless, breathless. Her face paled to the lips, while with wide, startled eyes she gazed on the impassive face before her. Then, " I do not understand you," she whispered.

" He is not dead."

The girl flung herself on the other, clutching at her. " Has he returned ? " she cried. " Have you seen him ? "

The foster-mother cast her off roughly. " I have seen him in a vision," she answered. " Last night in my dreams I saw him. The sound of the sea was in my ears, the wailing of the wind. He stood upon a rock, storm-tossed and forlorn, and I heard him call your name."

" But Alan—Alan has told me he is dead," the girl insisted.

" Alan ! " the other repeated scornfully. " I would as soon trust an adder as him."

" You wrong him," cried Ailsa indignantly.

" He loved Euar as we all did. Why should
he deceive us ? "

" You should know the answer to that
question. But go, I have warned you. And
do you warn the lover you have chosen that
one day Euar will return and pay the debt he
owes." Without another word she turned
and hurried away.

Ailsa stood for a moment or two wringing
her hands, shaken by the communication,
though knowing that it must come from the
distempered raving of one whom she counted
as insane. Utterly wretched she flung herself
on the sand and wept, hiding her face in her
hands.

So she lay when Alan found her and in great
anxiety asked the reason for her distress. He
started when Ailsa told him of the old woman's
vision ; but recovered himself in an instant
and laughed aside the suggestion of deception
or error on his part. " I would with all my
heart," he added, " that there were room for
doubt of Euar's death ; but there can be none.
We shall never see him again."

Nevertheless his wooing did not prosper
that morning; though he pleaded passionately
for an immediate marriage. Ailsa had
evidently not been quite unmoved by the old
woman's fantastic story and vowed that,
though she was willing to wed Alan, he must

N

wait for that event for a year and a day from the time of Euar's disappearance. And to that stipulation the lover had at length unwillingly to agree.

During the months which followed, the foster-mother was seldom seen abroad. The loss of Euar seemed to prey on her mind and embitter her nature. She had few friends and did not encourage those who would have shown neighbourly kindness to her. She was regarded as uncanny, and seemed rather to foster the fear that she inspired. She was often to be seen, in all weathers, prowling, solitary, around the coast, or standing, a gaunt figure against the sky-line of the cliffs, gazing out to sea. Ailsa and Alan both avoided her ; but she was not left entirely ignorant of their courtship, nor of the approach of their wedding day. At length the eve of that event arrived and brought an angry wind and driving rain. It was cold, too, and the lonely woman, crouching by her fire, sought to warm herself as she listened to the storm without, the howling of the gale, and the beating of the waves upon the distant shore.

The darkness deepened around her, relieved only by the flickering of the flames upon her hearth. She bent her face above them, gazing intently into the glowing embers, and muttering as if she read within them some

mysterious, lurid message. She sat motionless, except that at times she would fling back
impatiently a straying lock of grey hair as it
fell, interrupting her vision. Suddenly she
sprang to her feet, listening—a slow, heavy
footfall sounded from without and next
moment a loud knock fell upon the door.
With shaking limbs she fled to the entrance.
"Who is there?" she cried.

No answer came.

Trembling, she unfastened the latch, flung
the door wide, and looked out. A man stood
before her; but who or what he was she
could not see. "Who are you?" she asked.

A hoarse voice answered. "It is I, Euar.
Do you not know me?"

She flung herself on him, dragged him in,
laughing wildly, tears streaming the while
from her eyes. "I knew it," she cried, "I
saw your face in the embers. I heard the
winds call your name, O son of my heart!"
She would have fallen to the floor in her
paroxysm of excitement had he not upheld her.

But she rallied her strength. "Let me see
you," she continued. "Let me look upon
your face." And, breaking from his embrace,
she snatched up an armful of dried heather
and pitched it on the fire. On the instant it
blazed up illuminating the man before her, and
with a loud cry she recoiled from him; for

the face and form which she beheld were as none she had ever seen. From a matted tangle of hair, blackened features confronted her. His garments were in tatters. " You are not my Euar," she gasped.

" I am he," he laughed, and his tones were harsh as a raven's croak.

" I do not know your voice," she protested.

" How should you ? " he asked. " Since for how many months I cannot tell I have had none but sea birds to speak to."

" It cannot be . . ." she wailed.

" Mother ! Mother ! " he cried in an agony of mind, " you must know me ! "

Still she hesitated.

He reached forth his arms. " The sun has beaten on me ; winds and rain and the salt sea have lashed me ; how should I not change ? " He plucked at the plaid around him and, rotted, it rent in his grasp. " Do you not know my plaid ? " he asked. Then a sudden thought flashed. " My hose ? " he pointed. " All that is left of them—surely you know them, you who made them ? "

Instantly she knelt beside him gazing, fingering the worsted work with trembling fingers. " Yes, yes," she cried, " these are the hose I made, and you must be my Euar, my son, my son." She embraced his knees. " Tell me, tell me where you have been ? "

"From the day we parted," he told her, "I have been on the rocky island of Heisker miles out at sea, and not another foot than mine has been set on it since then."

"But Alan told us you were drowned."

"Curse on him!" cried Euar. "I have lived for Ailsa, and in the hope of my revenge on him. He left me there, sailed from me, leaving me to die. But I found a spring of fresh water to drink, and whelks to eat, and on these I have lived. A passing boat took me off but yesterday. I waited for night before returning here and have left my boat on the shore."

She arose to her feet. "Listen," she bade. "I have always known that black-hearted villain to be false; but how false he is, you don't yet know." And she told him of Alan and Ailsa's betrothal, and how they were to wed next morning.

He listened, and the fury of his anger seemed to inspire him with renewed strength. "Let me go quickly," he urged.

Suddenly she threw off the cap she had worn, allowing her grey hair to fall over her shoulders in wild disorder. She bared her knees and fell on them in the attitude of prayer. She raised her face. "The burning of his heart be to him," she cried. "The spell of his death stroke be his. Death without a priest to him.

I have made my wish before this and I will make it now, and there was not yet a day I did not see my wish fulfilled."

So terrible was the look on her face that Euar, for a moment, shrank from her, appalled; then, springing towards her, he pulled her to her feet. "Hush!" he bade. "This is no time for words. Let me go," and he would have dragged her from the hut.

But, exhausted and breathless from the paroxysm of her outburst though she was, she resisted him, and presently, recovering her composure, she forced him to eat and drink and put on fresh clothing; then together they went forth for Alan's house where revels were being held in anticipation of the wedding on the morrow. The night was dark; but the way was familiar to them and they needed no lantern to guide them. Within half an hour the twinkling lights of the dwelling they sought, shone before them.

Suddenly Euar stopped short, clasping his hand to his side. "My dirk!" he exclaimed, "I have forgotten it."

"You must return," the woman bade.

"No," he answered, "I shall find a weapon there."

Cautiously they approached, and heard the sounds of laughter and merry-making from within. Euar stood behind her while she knocked loudly on the door.   At the summons the laughter ceased and presently someone demanded who it was that stood without.

At the announcement of her name, the two who had waited on the threshold could hear the muttering of many voices as if in hurried discussion of this unwelcome visitor, but no words were audible.   Presently an agreement seemed to have been reached, for the door was pushed open, and, in the light which streamed forth, several men stood peering out into the night. " What seek you ? " one asked.

" I seek your hospitality," the woman answered, " both for myself and for a stranger who has come to me from a distant land."

" You have been no friend to Alan," one objected.

" I have come to make amends," she replied.

" And your companion ? " they questioned.

" He is sorely afflicted and cannot speak. Warmth and shelter for an hour—that is all I ask."

The men were still hesitating, when Alan, who had evidently overheard this conversation, came pressing his way past his companions. " Enough, enough," he laughed, " let them enter. None shall be denied welcome this night by Ailsa or me."

They stared at Euar's blackened face and

matted hair ; but with bowed head he kept himself as much as possible in the shade, avoiding their scrutiny. He had not failed, however, to observe Ailsa who stood at the far end of the room, and from her he never averted his covert gaze. She had started as her eyes first rested on him ; but, after a moment, her attention had been withdrawn. Two women and three of Alan's kinsmen were gathered there, eating cakes and drinking ale. They pressed the visitors to share these refreshments ; but they refused. So, after many hospitable efforts were found to be unavailing, the wedding party ignored these unresponsive guests.

Peaceable though the occasion was, the foster-mother had noted that all the men were yet armed, and never for a moment had she relaxed her watchfulness for an opportunity to provide Euar with a weapon. Chance favoured her. The merriment had waxed fast and furious—bride and bridegroom with their friends were about to dance, and for the purpose furniture was thrust aside. In the upheaval a rude bedstead near which she was standing was removed, disclosing a heap of articles which had been concealed beneath it, and amongst these a bow and a sheaf of arrows —Euar's long lost bow ! She knew it at a glance. Unseen, she kicked both aside into

a dark corner where they might lie hidden from
view.   To the music of the pipes the dancers
stepped and flung, until, panting for breath,
they paused to rest.

" The loving cup," cried one, referring to the
large beaker containing ale which, in accor-
dance with ancient custom, was passed on such
occasions from lip to lip.

The cup was immediately handed to the
bride, who sipped it and passed it on.   From
one to another it circulated until only Euar
was left.   Ailsa was watching him and for a
moment he met her troubled gaze ; but in that
moment she saw him drop something in the
vessel.   No other had seen his action ; none
looked within the cup as it was returned
whence it came.   But when it was once more
within her grasp she snatched from its interior
a gold ring.   One glance sufficed to tell her
it was the betrothal token she herself had given
to Euar—the symbol of her love !   The faint
whisper of fleeting suspicion became in an
instant the clamour of conviction.   Euar had
returned, changed beyond recognition he stood
before her now.   Faintness overwhelmed her.
The lights, the faces of those assembled seemed
to swim around her.   They saw her pale, sway,
as if about to fall, and rushed to her aid ; but
panting she thrust them back, pointing to the

stranger who only stood aloof. "Euar," she cried. "It is Euar who stands there!"

They turned to stare incredulously at the man thus identified, and for a moment no one moved. But next instant Euar himself sprang into the light, standing behind a table. "Yes," he shouted, pointing towards Alan, "it is I, Euar, whom that false traitor left to die on Heisker. Let him answer to me now."

Still not a man moved, but like a flash the foster-mother leaped to the door and flung it wide. "Escape, escape for your life," she screamed.

Weaponless Euar stood; but not resource-less; for he saw the purpose in Alan's flaming eyes, and with one mighty heave overturned the table on the men as they sprang at him. They floundered in confusion on the floor; while, with a shout of defiance and derision, he darted to the door, snatched the bow and arrows held out to him by his foster-mother and was gone into the night.

With a piercing cry Ailsa had fallen senseless to the floor, but none paid heed to her. The other women clung together; the men strove to recover their footing. The first to do so sprang to the doorway from which a long beam of light penetrated far into the darkness; he thrust aside the foster-mother who would have intercepted him, stood for a moment uncertain

whither to turn, the next, leaped into the air
and fell prostrate, transfixed by an arrow.
Two other pursuers followed, stumbling over
the fallen body, and, ere they could arise, they
too were pierced, and pitched headlong. Of
the men, Alan, only, now remained. He had
seen the fate of his kinsmen, and sought, by
cunning, himself to avoid it. Standing in
concealment he suddenly threw his plaid
through the open door, and, as an arrow sped
through it, and before another could follow, he
leaped with a shout into the darkness and ran.
But next instant fingers like steel closed about
his throat and he fell backward with Euar on
the top of him. He snatched his dirk ; but it
was torn form his grasp and plunged again and
again into his writhing body until he lay
forever still.

Suddenly before the eyes of the terrified
women within the house, the wild and blood-
stained form of Euar stood and gazed around.
He saw Ailsa where she lay, and rushing forward, seized her in his arms, and, without a
word, bore her out.

His foster-mother followed, entreating him
to stop ; but he paid no heed, hurrying with
his burden through the night. Panting,
stumbling, she pursued him, on and on,
still unable to overtake him, weighted though
he was. He never turned, never spoke.

The clouds had rolled aside and moonlight shone. She saw him reach the shore at length, and the waiting boat dimly descried in the half light. Laying the unconscious girl on board he pushed forth the little craft. He leaped into it, seized the oars and rowed further and further out to sea.

"Euar, Euar," the distracted woman called his name; but he did not seem to hear. She watched until night and the heaving waste of waters veiled him from her view. Into their mystery he had vanished to be seen or heard of never again.

RESCUE.

Am fear nach eisd ris nach toigh leis
Cha'n fhaic e na 's fhearr leis.

He who will not listen to what he does not like
Will not see what will please him.

"DO not leave me, Martin," she entreated. He knelt by her bedside, clasping the white hand she had stretched towards him and kissing it tenderly. "Sweetheart," he answered, "no harm can come to you, and I shall hasten like a deer. Old Margaret will return quickly. She is wise and will know what you need. For your own sake I must go."

"Wait only until to-morrow," she pleaded, "I shall be better then."

"But you said so yesterday, and still you are ill."

"I am afraid, Martin."

"What is there to fear? No one ever comes to this glen—I wish to Heaven they would, and then you would be less lonely than you are! I had no right to take you from your home and friends to this solitude—you who used to be so gay. I have done you a great wrong."

" Now it is you who are foolish," she smiled through her tears. " You know very well indeed that I would rather be here alone with you than with all the other people in the world. And besides," she lifted a corner of her blanket as she spoke, disclosing the tiny face of the week-old infant by her side. "You forget him," she added.

He looked fondly at his little son sleeping peacefully on the young mother's arm. " No," he corrected, " I was thinking you have a great champion there to keep you from harm."

The look of anxiety, which for a moment had passed, now returned to the mother's eyes as they were raised towards her husband's face. " But it is for him I fear," she said.

" But didn't old Margaret tell you she had never seen a healthier boy ? " he asked.

She looked fearfully around and, motioning him to bend low his ear, " Listen ! " she whispered. " It is no sickness for him that I dread. It is the little folk, the people of peace ! "*

" These are only foolish tales," he laughed,

But in terror she bade him be silent, lest he should anger the beings of whom she had spoken. Not for the first time did she refer to them. When he had brought her as his bride,

* The Fairies.

little over a year before, to the desolate glen where his shepherd's cottage stood, she had observed the knoll a few hundred yards from their door—the knoll that was ever green, where in spring the primroses clustered, and in summer the hair-bells and fern drooped, where the birds seemed to sing most sweetly. Ah, the beautiful knoll with the tumbling, ever murmuring burn by its side !

She had seen it and clapped her hands, like the happy girl she was, and had drawn him to her side that she might whisper that this surely was a dwelling-place of the peaceful people.

And sometimes, as time passed on summer evenings, she would tell him guardedly of how, sitting there, she had heard the patter of little feet and the faint sounds of singing, and music too delightful to be that of mortals, echoing, echoing softly from somewhere underground.

And always he had tried to laugh away her fancies, telling her that only in imagination had she seemed to hear these signs of elfin life. And so she had ceased to speak of them. He had even believed that she had forgotten the dangerous subject, and therefore it was with regret that now he heard her refer to it again.

No doubt the great ordeal through which she had so lately passed had left her weak and imaginative, the more so that, though the old woman, Margaret, who had attended her, had returned to her own cottage two miles distant believing that she was no longer required, during the previous day the young mother had been feverish and obviously in need of more attention than could be given by her husband. So he had determined that Margaret must be recalled. As for his wife's dread of the peaceful folk—Highlander though he was—he had never shared her belief in their existence. He himself had never seen or heard them, and though it was said that new-born babes and their mothers were especially liable to be captured by these malicious beings, still, even supposing such stories to be true, there were safeguards which could be adopted. In any case, if risk there were in leaving his wife and child alone, the risk of delaying for her the old woman's ministrations seemed greater. Not for another hour would he wait; so, as gently as might be, he declared his determination.

And Julia, his wife, realising that she could not shake his resolution, pleaded no more. All her thoughts were for the child lying there so helpless, asleep. But it was for the mother that Martin's care was exercised, the young wife whom he loved with all the intensity of his being. To humour her he would leave his naked dirk lying on her bosom; for was not steel held to be a thing of dread to the still folk?

Steel or iron, it was said, they dared not approach. And, comforted by the knowledge of the potency of the metal, she smiled at him as he kissed her farewell and tenderly smoothed her pillow—the great, strong husband of hers, her very own man.

He turned for a moment in the doorway to look at her once more—her dear face so pale, but so beautiful, so young, so like that of a child, with the auburn locks around it, smiling bravely still.

"Quick, Martin," she bade.

He hesitated. Should he stay? Was there indeed danger in leaving her thus? He glanced without. The glen lay bathed in the splendour of the setting sun. The great majestic hills towered around, purple in the evening rays, as if clothed in royal robes of light, steadfast, protective. Not a breath stirred the air. Silence, save for the peaceful crooning of the burn at hand. He saw the knoll. It was arrayed in verdure as it had ever been. He could hear a robin pipe its tiny melody from the hazel bushes there. Far up in the blue an eagle soared. Not a human being was in sight.

"Quick, Martin."

He hesitated no longer. With one hasty wave of his hand he turned and left her, closed the door gently behind him, whistled to his

o

dog which lay basking in the sunlight, and ran down the pathway, the dog bounding gleefully before him. His course lay by the water side, up the glen. Alternately running and walking he could cover the distance in a quarter of an hour, though no path was there to hasten his progress. He reached the knoll, and for a second paused to stare at its greenery. Not a whisper broke the stillness, no blade of grass or fern-frond stirred. A rabbit suddenly bolted from cover at his feet and scurried to a burrow, vainly pursued with yelps by the dog. He called his animal to him and hurried on. Why had he not left the dog with her? He would have been protection. She believed that fairy folk dreaded dogs. Too late now. Through bracken and heather he sped, now on this side the burn, now bounding over to the other, as obstructions seemed the less. The moor-fowl arose clamorously from the hill-sides at his approach. Once a hare stole before him and then, breaking cover, bounded up the hill as easily as if on level ground, paused a while to watch him, and then more leisurely continued its career, while Martin ignored the evil omen.*

Trained as a mountaineer, tirelessly, and with amazing rapidity, Martin hurried on with

---

* A hare crossing one's path means bad luck.

ever the thought of Julia's sweet, pale face before him. She would be counting the minutes awaiting his return.

The cottage at length, where old Margaret lived with her grandson—a shepherd like himself. The clamour of a dog announcing the approach of a stranger, and Margaret herself, standing in the doorway of the rude, thatched dwelling, shading her eyes as she peered down the path. She pushed the dog within, closing the door on it, recognising her visitor, and came hastening to meet him—a little, bright-eyed old woman. " And what is it that brings you here to me, Martin ? " she asked. " Is it the sweet lassie or the bonnie babe that needs me ? "

" It is Julia that will be needing you this night, Margaret," he answered her ; " though sorry I am to trouble you."

" And what trouble would I not gladly take for that lass ? It is you that is the lucky man, Martin, to have her as your wife. But tell me what is the matter ? "

Briefly he informed her of the condition in which Julia lay.

" Aye," she answered, " I will come with you this very minute. Hamish (her grandson) will understand." She was as incapable of writing a message as would Hamish have been of reading it, but as a sign of her departure and the direction in which she had gone, she found an old shoe and left it on the table, its toe pointing down the glen.

Though of school education she had none, nevertheless Margaret was recognised by all in that sparsely populated district as a wise woman. She was in great request, not only in cases such as that of Julia, but in times of trouble in general. She could tell by touching one who was sick whether that person would recover, and she was skilful in forecasting events by examining the shoulder-blade of a sheep, or by other generally recognised methods of divination.

She was a kindly soul, too, and had formed a deep attachment to Julia, and therefore it was with real concern that she accompanied Martin on his homeward way. But she was old and frail, and quite unable to hasten with the rapidity with which he would have covered the distance had he been alone. She had often to pause to recover her breath, and there were also long intervals of delay, when the burn had to be crossed. Martin curbed his impatience as best he could, but he was tormented by anxieties and a vague sense of impending disaster. The sun had set, but the long summer twilight of Beltane's Eve* softly

* The first night of summer when fairies have power.

lit the landscape, and silence had fallen on all the world asleep, save for the restless burn.

Not a word had either said concerning danger from the peaceful folk to the young mother and her child; but that the subject was not far from Margaret's mind one incident on their way bore evidence. They had just passed the knoll and were within sight of the cottage. It stood before them apparently undisturbed, all as it had been when left by Martin. Hens were still scraping about the door, and a couple of ducks emerged, at the moment, waddling from the burn. Not a breath stirred the air ; but suddenly down the pathway towards them came a whirling eddy of wind, tossing and twining upward stray withered grass of the past winter. Silently yet swiftly the spirals swept upon them, while amazed they paused to gaze. The dog sprang backward, barking furiously ; but Margaret flung herself on Martin, gasping in agitation and dismay. "The folk !" she exclaimed, "the still folk ! " See, they pass. Throw your dirk at them. Quick ! Quick ! "

Startled by her outburst Martin frowned at her, but next instant laughed, and, to humour her, felt for his dirk and would have thrown it as he was bidden ; but he felt in vain—he had left the weapon at home. " I have nothing to throw," he told her.

Still clutching his arm, but silently now, Margaret turned with him and together they watched the eddy whirl over the bank and up the glen until it reached the knoll, and there it seemed to die away. The wise old woman understood the significance of that phenomenon. Was it not so that fairies bore their captives from the human race? Iron or steel thrown at them as they passed would have forced them to relinquish their prize; but it was too late now. "Your wife and the babe," she cried, and loosing her hold on Martin she fled towards the cottage.

He knew what she feared, but would not share her belief; yet for a moment he turned again, gazing at the knoll suffused by the tender twilight, sweet and peaceful. Not a leaf of its hazel bushes moved; not a blade of grass stirred. He heard the robin still pipe its tiny, silver song. And yet his heart beat quickly as if agitated by a sudden cold breath of fear. Next instant he was racing madly after Margaret. In a few strides he overtook her, passed her. The ducks and hens fled clamorously from him, but he paid no heed to them. The door stood ajar. He noticed that with a shock; for he knew he had left it closed. He burst within and stood. Despite the semi-darkness, one glance showed him that his wife was not in her bed. The blanket had

been tossed aside from where she had lain.
Terror seized him. "Julia," he shouted and,
rushing forward, flung back the bed clothes
and revealed his baby sleeping peacefully,
the dirk laid over it; but not his wife.
"Julia," he frantically called her name again
and gazed wildly around. But only old
Margaret came to his call, stumbling into the
room in her haste, hurrying towards him.
"She's gone," he gasped, "she's gone!"

The old woman fluttered to the bed, bent
over, and plucked the dirk from the sleeping
child. "You left that on him?" she asked.

"No, on her."

"She must have moved it then, protecting
her baby, and left herself at their mercy."

"I won't believe it," he cried in agonised
tones. "They can't have taken her. There
are no such beings."

Margaret flung up a warning hand.
"Hush!" she whispered, "you are mad to
speak as you do. You will only anger them
the more."

But with an impatient gesture he turned
from her. "I will find her yet," he declared,
"though Hell itself should try to hide her
from me!" And leaving Margaret with the
child he rushed headlong from the house.
A cow-shed stood near. She might be in
concealment there. He flung himself within;

but only the lowing and rightful occupant turned her head; no human being could he find. He raced around the peat-stacks— nothing. Bewildered, distraught, he gazed about him, but saw only the familiar landscape —the shadowed hills and glen, not a sign of any living soul. "Julia, Julia!" he called aloud in his despair. Only the echoes flung back her name, as if in mockery. The knoll! There it stood. He glared at it. Was there indeed menace beneath its verdant repose? Could these tales be true? He would test their alleged truth at all cost. Without further hesitation he ran resolutely to the spot, burst his way through the obstructing bushes and bracken, tearing his clothes, stumbling, but never pausing until breathless he stood upon the sward which crowned the summit. Except for a thrush which broke cover and flew with loud expostulations from his intrusion on its sanctuary, nothing stirred, no sound or movement, absolute stillness; only the throbbing of his heart and pulses. He stamped on the ground. "If there are beings within this hill, let them hear me," he cried aloud. "If you have taken my wife from me, give her back, or I shall dig your haunts down though I spend the remainder of my life on the work." He listened—no answer, only a faint breeze stirred the leaves

beneath him, as if a whispering voice had
tremulously breathed his name. Suddenly
his rage gave place to nameless dread, and he
shook as if with palsy.

He flung himself face downward on the
ground. "My darling, my darling! Are you
there?" he cried. Perhaps it was but the
note of a bird; but to him it seemed like a
chuckle of derisive mirth behind him. He
leaped to his feet. "Who is there?" he
shouted—silence again. "There is nothing,
nothing," he cried, "all is madness." And,
leaping down the descent, he forced his way
through the bushes again, and ran towards his
deserted home.

Margaret met him on the threshold, the baby
in her arms, pointing, "Look!" she cried.

He saw only a duck, which expecting, no
doubt, to be fed, came boldly towards her.

"What do you mean?" he demanded
fiercely.

"It is an omen," she answered in great
excitement. "Aye, an omen of good. She
will return to you, Martin; all will yet be
well!" *

"I care nothing for your omens," he told
her, and would have turned aside.

She gazed at the terrible look in his eyes;

---

* A duck approaching a seer indicated the return of one
who had been lost.

then held the baby out to him. "Take him," she bade. But he did not seem to hear.

"He is Julia's child," she reminded him. "She would wish you to think of him."

Still he neither spoke nor moved.

"I must find a foster-mother for him," she continued; "though where, God knows. Poor, helpless little one!" She laid the child on his arm.

He looked at his little son and something like a sob seemed to choke him.

"You must feed him as best you can;" Margaret bade. "You'll find a bowl of milk within. I shall return as quickly as I am able."

Mechanically Martin carried the child within and laid it in a cot by the empty bed; but he could not rest. He was certain Julia had not gone up the glen; but it was possible that in fevered delirium she might have wandered down. Unobserved by Margaret, who was speeding homeward, he hurried in the opposite direction, determined to reach the nearest dwelling there—three miles distant. But neither with the neighbours whom he sought, nor on the way was he rewarded. The night was well advanced when, exhausted and with haggard face, he re-entered his cottage there to find the child, wailing indeed, but unharmed. He made some clumsy attempts to feed it with a spoon, and then flung himself on the bed. But he could not sleep. Hour after hour he lay, while tormenting thoughts haunted his mind, and with the first red streaks of dawn he was up again. Until Margaret's return he dared not leave the child for long ; but all that day he wandered up and down, without food, without rest, re-entering his house only at intervals. But no sooner was he within than he would seem to hear whispering voices, as if there were those who lurked furtively near, and were peeping and spying upon him from the lintel of the door or through the window. And with frenzied haste he would rush out to find, at one time, swallows skimming from his approach, at another, wisps of straw blown hither and thither by the wind. As night again approached, midsummer though it was, he felt deadly cold, so he heaped the peats upon the fire which he had maintained that he might warm the baby's milk. For a time he crouched before the blaze, and in the embers seemed to see Julia's face looking at him with appealing eyes. Again he stretched himself on the bed, and again for hours he lay wakeful. At length, however, he must have dozed, for, as in a restless dream, he was aware that the child cried. Suddenly, however, the weeping ceased and the silence awakened him. All was still, save for a faint sound monotonously repeated, a soothing sound, such as might proceed from the gentle rocking of a chair. For a moment he remained listening. Then, wondering drowsily, he opened his eyes. Even at midnight, in that summer time, a gray light was diffused from the northern sky and fell, ghostly, through the little window. From the hearth the embers, too, still shed a fitful glow. Someone was seated before them, someone who held the baby in her arms and rocked to and fro, crooning very softly to the sleeping child. It was Julia. He saw her long, auburn hair streaming over her shoulders. He caught glimpses of her dear, familiar face. Was he dreaming? Had all been a dream, a dreadful dream of her absence? His heart leaped wildly and then seemed to stand still. He felt paralysed, hardly able to breathe. Then he heard her sing, but so low that her song too might have been but a dream :

" Hush-a-bye, hush-a-bye, little babe, lonely,
    Left in the darkness, of shadows afraid !
    Hush baby, hush !   Nought can harm you while only
    Enfolded and safe in my arms you are laid.

" Softly I'll sing to you, sweet, lest you waken,
    Charming your dreams with the fairy refrain
    That from blue-bells a-droop in the twilight is shaken,
    Arousing from slumbers the fairies again.

" Whisper of leaves and all sounds that enrapture,
    Patter of rain-drops, or silvery dew,
    Bubbles that float from the burn I shall capture
    And toss them aloft, in your dreaming, for you.

" Soon comes the fairy call, faint but compelling,
    Bidding me glide, as the moonbeams, on air
    To the glamour-enchantment and gleam of their dwell-
        ing
    Where the false seems the true and the foul is the fair."

Silence. If this were a dream, any movement or word from him might break it, and
it might never, never come again. Yet he
could not refrain from whispering : " Julia."

Slowly she turned her face to him and smiled.

Trembling, still as if in a trance, he arose
and with out-stretched arms moved towards
her. But she, too, stood and receded from
his advance. With a loud cry he sprang to
enfold her in his arms and found—emptiness.
She was gone ! He staggered, bewildered,
looking about him. The baby lay peacefully
asleep in its cot, but not another soul than himself and the child was there. The door stood
slightly ajar. He had not noticed that before.
The moon had arisen and a narrow beam fell
glittering on his dirk. Picking it up he rushed
out, looking hither and thither, straining his
ears for the sound of a foot-fall. And then,
like the sigh of the night wind in the heather,
his name, " Martin, Martin." And yonder,

yonder! Was that a wreath of mist from the burn, floating in the moonlight? Or a woman's form that seemed to drift farther and farther from his gaze towards the fairy hill? She was being borne from him. She was calling to him for help. "I am coming, I am coming," he shouted, and rushed madly in pursuit.

In after days he could remember only vaguely what ensued. Strange voices seemed to call him, now from this quarter, now from that, as if to perplex and mislead him; mocking laughter assailed his ears. A sudden tempest arose and angry winds buffeted him. Monstrous shapes, distorted things, loomed menacingly from the night about him, plucking at him. But on he sped, stumbling and again recovering himself. Sometimes he felt as if an icy cold were freezing the very blood within his veins; and then hot breath, as from a furnace-flame, scorched and raged upon him. Suddenly a great silence fell, and darkness, complete and awful, and he felt weighted as with lead. Hardly could he drag one foot after the other. Somehow he felt— for he could not see—that he was entering a mighty portal. An iron door swung ponderously from his strength. What if it should close forever behind him? A memory awoke. Steel or iron, steel or iron could defeat all magic power. He felt for and found a crevice and, thrusting the point of his dirk into it, left the weapon quivering there. Cavernous regions seemed to yawn beyond, engulfing him; but he pressed onwards until, at length, to his intense relief, a faint ray of light met his gaze—brighter, brighter.

He could see the shadows of vast rocks and he knew that he had penetrated far beneath the surface of the earth. The light shone from a quarter concealed from his view by an abrupt turn of the subterranean way and as he approached, overwhelming dread assailed him. He knew not what appalling spectacle might confront him there. The utter silence was fearful. He fought back the terror that shook him, and painfully, step by step, advanced. He turned the corner, looked, and a cry of amazement rang from his lips, for he seemed to see the room of his own dwelling, the very room he had left but a few minutes past. The fire still smouldered on the hearth —the table, the bed, the crib, but no baby was there. And there, on her chair sat Julia, his own Julia, asleep. He sprang towards her, kneeling by her side, clasping her; but she neither answered him nor stirred—impassive, lifeless. Was she dead? He gazed wildly on her. No, not dead, surely not dead; for though her face was still pale, it was the face of the living. He would lift her and bear her in his arms, carry her from this place of enchantment, away, away until continents separated them from it, and then all would be well with her again. But, strive as he might, he could not move her. Perhaps his strength, too, was being charmed away. Perhaps he, too, would presently sink into impotent oblivion. Agony, agony! Darkness,—the light was failing. And singing, voices singing. Music that would steal his soul. He would see Julia no more. But one last farewell. One last kiss. He stooped, pressed his lips to hers. And then—wonder of wonders—she opened her eyes. She smiled. She sprang into his arms, and straining her to his breast, he fled blindly, desperately, and —he remembered no more.

*   *   *   *   *

A feeling of deadly weakness and languor. He was content to lie with closed eyes and listen to the pleasant sounds which met his ears—the song of a kettle boiling on the hearth, a cock crowing without. He could recall nothing of past events, could not think. Delicious impassivity. But presently a soft, cool hand was laid on his brow, smoothing aside his hair, and he looked up to find Julia's face bent anxiously above him.

And she, seeing recognition in his look,

knelt suddenly and whispered betwixt laughter and tears, "Thank God, thank God."

"What has happened?" he asked.

"Hush, hush," she bade, "you are better now and will soon be well."

And then memories began slowly to return—the horrors of that enchanted cave! He struggled feebly to arise. "The cave," he gasped, "Did I carry you safely out?"

Suddenly Margaret's face smiled over Julia's shoulder. Margaret, bearing his little son within her arms. "See!" She held the baby up. "See what a great fellow is here."

But still he wanted to know all that had befallen since that last frantic rush for freedom. "But how did I come here?" he asked.

And they, seeing that he would not rest until he knew all, told him how Margaret, hastening to them that eventful night, had found them together by the burn—Julia, still weak indeed, but in a measure recovered from the fever which had clouded her mind and driven her roaming amongst the hills as she herself declared. And Martin must have found her and had been bearing her homewards when exhaustion overwhelmed him and he had sunk fainting to the ground. They had not been far from the cottage and, somehow, Margaret

P

had contrived to convey him home. She had nursed him, and for a time, Julia too ; but the girl had recovered quickly. For ten days Martin had lain unconscious. Now all anxiety had ended.

He tried to tell them the truth concerning his rescue of Julia ; but, strange to say, they, who had previously so dreaded the peaceful folk, now refused to believe in their agency in recent events ; while he, who had scorned what he held to be superstition, now affirmed that only supernatural powers could account for the dangers which had beset him. His convictions were confirmed one day long after his recovery. He had refused to set foot again on the fairy hill, but Julia had no such timidity : she often pulled the wild flowers there. She had been so engaged on one occasion while he sat on the bank before their cottage. She came hastening towards him and held out to him his dirk, weather-stained, rusty.

" My dirk ! " he cried, " where did you find it ? "

" You must have lost it on the hill of the Folk," she answered ; " for I found it there with its point fixed within a crevice of the rocks."

THE WATER HORSE.

Is minig a bha 'n donas dàicheil.

The Devil is often attractive.

SOMETIMES on summer nights when the moon was shining you might have seen her sitting on the hillside above the loch, and at first you might not have known whether a woman crouched there, or whether that dim shape were but a wreath of mist, until you heard her sing. But the song you could not have mistaken, though its words, if words there were, were of no human language —just a strange intermingling of liquid sounds, ever fluctuating, changing, to be overborne at length by a refrain of overwhelming sadness.

Indeed all travellers by the loch-side, hearing that song, would hurry past and be glad to reach the shelter and security of their homes ; for it was well known that though mad Mary was gentle and harmless, yet her singing had in it something of the magical which it were better that a man should not hear.

Even in the daytime, few ever spoke to her— the solitary woman with her grey locks blown about the pale pinched face with its great wild eyes which roved ever to and fro—that face which once had been the fairest in all the Highlands. But, however much folk might fear her, none ever dared to meddle with or slight her. Even the children, though they fled from her approach, never ventured to taunt or jeer, for though they dreaded her, yet greater still was their terror of the vengeance of Calum Mor, her father, of Big Fair John, Middle Fair John, and Young Fair John, her brothers. From these relatives, rough and formidable though they were, she was always assured of tenderness.

In the little farm with its new house at the north end of the loch they lived secluded. Hardly ever a visitor passed their threshold; none was invited. Not that the family was poor; for Calum had always prospered in material affairs, shrewd and hard-working as he and his three stalwart sons were; nor had they always been unsociable. The day had been when Calum's dwelling was the scene of many a hospitable gathering; and the cup had circulated merrily while the roof had rung with sounds of song and laughter. But then his wife had been alive and Mary was the maiden for whom half the lads in the neighbourhood were ready to fly at each other's throats, dirk in hand.

No greater contrast could have been found

at that time than that presented between Mary and the men of her family. Calum himself was big and boisterous, and very unlike the morose and taciturn man he became after the awful event which was destined to deprive his daughter of her reason. He was by nature jovial, and, though of a violent temper when roused, was usually not without just reason for the outburst. He was an honest man and as such was held in respect.

His three sons were big and burly like their father, but, though sharing something of his vehemence of temperament, were lacking in his sagacity. They were shy of strangers, all very devoted to one another, content with the domestic life which their home afforded them.

Mary, in the days of which this story tells, was about eighteen years of age and as vivacious as her father and brothers were reserved—merry and gay, with a sweet voice which could be heard often in the plaintive songs she loved to sing. She was fond of companionship and her lovely eyes would sparkle and her laughter ring like silver bells as, with other girls of her own age, she bantered the awkward youths who came a-courting them. But, for a time, they courted her in vain. Much though she loved the society of her friends, occasions were frequent when she seemed to prefer solitude. Often she would steal away alone to the hills and sit in the heather, listening to the larks singing ; or she would wander up the burns, picking the wild flowers from the banks. Most of all, however, she delighted in lying by the loch, lulled by the gentle lap of the waters on the pebbles of the shore, and, with half-shut eyes, dream long, sweet dreams—innocent fancies of which none but she ever knew. Sometimes she would remain there for hours together, until the purple shadows deepened in the glen and cold mists arose, floating and drifting in fantastic wreaths over the unruffled surface of the darkly sleeping waters. Only when her name was loudly called by one of her brothers sent in search of her, would she awake from her reverie and run homewards.

With the arrival of young Alister a happier destiny seemed about to dawn for Mary ; for from their first meeting they loved each other. His parents had formerly lived there ; but, shortly after his birth, had left the neighbourhood. Both were now dead and the young man had returned to reside with an uncle, whose little farm he would one day inherit. Alister was therefore eligible and, in addition, was as fine and handsome a lad as any maiden might covet as husband. The match seemed in every way suitable and was highly approved by Calum, his wife, and their sons who welcomed the prospect of this addition, in the person of Alister, to their family. The lovers were therefore formally betrothed and the wedding day fixed ; but just when all the horizon of their lives seemed cloudless, suddenly the prospect was overcast : Mary's mother was seized with sickness and lay dying. They tended her with every care ; but all their efforts were unavailing and a night at length came when they knew that the end was near. Husband, sons, and daughter were gathered by the bed of the dying woman. A summer's day had ended and darkness was deepening without and within the room where she lay ; but they lit no light, grouped there in the dark, Calum kneeling, his great shoulders bowed over the frail hand that was slowly growing cold within his grasp. Mary, too, knelt by his side. Her brothers stood. The mother's breathing had seemed to cease. She lay without movement. They wondered whether she were already dead ; when suddenly her eyes opened. She turned her face towards Mary. "Alister," she whispered. "Bring Alister to me."

It was Young Fair John who sped on her errand, and, in less time than had seemed possible, he was back again, bringing Alister with him.

Mary leaned forward. "Alister is here, Mother, dearest," she announced.

The dying woman opened her eyes and feebly motioned the young man to approach. She took his hand and laid it on that of Mary. "She is a sweet lass," she whispered. "Guard her well."

"With my life, if need be," he answered her.

She looked long and wistfully in his face. "Aye," she said, "you are a good lad and will make her happy. Fain would I have seen you both with the bonny children about your knees; but that is not to be." Then her lips moved inaudibly, perhaps in prayer. Not a sound broke the stillness. All were waiting. Suddenly she sat up, gazing with wide eyes on Alister and pointing a shaking hand. "Beware!" she cried. "Do not touch, do not go near it!" Her eyes wandered and seemed to be following in her imagination some fearful scene, while all who were around her shrank from her, aghast and helpless. She spoke again in agonised accents: "Swifter, swifter. O God! Can no one stop him? It is a monster, a thing of terror. Plunge a dirk, a knife in it!" Her voice rose to a wail of dismay. "Too late, too late!" She paused, rocking herself to and fro as if unable longer to endure the spectacle which her delirium had conjured before her eyes. For a minute or

two she remained thus, moaning as if in
anguish, and then again she looked up. "His
plaid!" she whispered. "His plaid upon the
water and . . . and underneath . . . . ."
With one piercing shriek she fell forward,
dead, upon the bed.

But in their grief they forgot her ill-omened
and prophetic vision until, later, circumstances
recalled it with terrible reality to their memory.

As a consequence of her mother's death
Mary's wedding was postponed, and for a time
she was inconsolable; not even Alister being
able to comfort her; though day after day
he came to the farm and by his gentleness and
by constant and thoughtful little attentions
sought to distract her melancholy thoughts.
But though she thanked him and tried to smile
in his honest, troubled eyes, she would often
make her escape, preferring to wander alone
with her grief. And always it was by the
loch-side that she sat, gazing out silently over
the face of the waters.

One evening, about a fortnight after
the mother's funeral, Big Fair John, Mary's
eldest brother, was returning from the
hills skirting the loch when, to his surprise,
he found his sister accompanied by a young
man. They were sitting together on a
knoll and talking so earnestly that at first
they did not observe the approach of the

brother. Big Fair John stopped and stared in amazement. Mary's companion was a stranger of unusual appearance with long, black hair flung back from a face of extraordinary pallor. He had large dark eyes which, as they rested on the girl, seemed to flash and glow like the reflection of a burning sunset from the loch. He was dressed in garments of green and was clumsily shod in leather shoes.

" Who is this ? " asked Big Fair John, none too pleased to find his sister conversing with this unknown person.

The youth at once rose to his feet, smiling and bowing to the surly questioner. " I am a stranger who has journeyed here. I have lost my way," he answered. "This maid was most kindly directing me."

Big Fair John noted the young man's voice —unlike any other he had ever heard. It was muffled and guttural, with occasional high inflexions. Speaking afterwards of it he described it as being like the drip of oozing slime —something to shudder at.

" What is your name ? " he demanded gruffly.

" My name," the other answered, " you would not know it if I were to tell it."

" What do you seek ? "

" Only freedom to wander for a while with nothing above me but the sky, to breathe

the air and to leap light as the wind over the
heather."

The more Big Fair John looked at and
listened to the young man the less he liked
him.   " Well then," said he, "since you seek
nothing from us, you had better be gone ;
the more so that we do not care to have
nameless strangers loitering around."

The youth laughed.

Big Fair John started, for the laugh stirred
memories, though of what he could not recall.

" You speak truly," the stranger continued.
" The time has come when I must return
whence I came."   He turned towards Mary.
" I go," he added ; " but we shall meet again."
Without another word he walked away from
them.

They stood watching him and noticed that
though his form seemed lithe and agile he yet
moved awkwardly, as if both his feet were
lame.   When at length he passed from sight
round the shoulder of a hill, Big Fair John
drew a sigh of relief and turning a wrathful
face upon his sister, " I think it hardly
maidenly," he rebuked, " that you should
talk with a stranger like that."

But Mary only tossed her head; and so in
silence they continued their way homeward.

During the following days Mary's dejection
seemed to deepen ; she appeared to be pre-

occupied and dazed, as if moving in a dream. She had lost all the light-hearted gaiety, which formerly had lent to her such charm, and she became silent and listless, often sitting for hours together with folded hands and fixed gaze. Her father naturally attributed this alteration to grief for her mother's death, and, though full of sympathy for her, tried with rough kindliness to arouse her; but in vain. Poor Alister was greatly upset by her demeanour towards him. She acquiesced in his presence; but she no longer welcomed him as she had done. She seemed to be indifferent whether he were with her or not. The anxiety of her family on her behalf was, however, greatly increased one morning.

All night Calum had tossed and turned, tormented by disturbing dreams and therefore, wearying of his unrefreshing rest, he arose before daybreak to attend to an ailing ewe. The house was in complete silence. The embers on the hearth glowed feebly; but saving from these, no light shone.

Something prompted him to pause by Mary's room and on reaching out a hand he was surprised to find that the door stood wide open. He listened—no sound of breathing could be heard. Somehow he felt uneasy and stepped within. "Mary," he whispered

—no answer. Again, but this time louder, he called her name. Still she did not reply. He stepped towards her bed, and found it unoccupied. Alarmed, he hastened to where Big Fair John was soundly sleeping, awakened him, and told him of Mary's absence. A whispered conversation followed in which agreement was reached to disturb as yet no other member of the family, and five minutes later father and son rushed out into the gray of early dawn to be confronted immediately by Mary herself returning. But to the vehement questions put to her she could return no satisfactory answers. She seemed bewildered, half awake, and declared with tears that she could not tell why she had gone out, had, indeed, no recollection of doing so, and believed that she must have wandered from the house in her sleep.

Father and brothers were now seriously anxious on the girl's account, and Alister was in the greatest distress. It seemed to them that her mind was affected, that madness threatened her. And sitting together they discussed what was to be done. It was Calum who at length suggested that, if Alister were willing, he should marry her without further delay. But he, though eager for the wedding, declared that only with Mary's concurrence would he agree to the plan. They decided, therefore, that he himself should broach this project to her.

Mary sat by the fire alone when, next day, Alister entered the house and, standing by her side, took her listless hand. "Mary," he addressed her.

She gazed silently at him with vacant eyes as if she failed to recognise him.

He knelt beside her. "Mary," he implored, "tell me what has changed you so. Something more than your mother's death weighs on your mind. There is no sorrow that I would not willingly share with you. Tell me —do you love me still?"

She looked fearfully around as if dreading an unseen listener. "Hush! hush!" she bade.

"Whom do you fear?" he asked. "There is no one else here."

She gazed at him as if struggling to awake from a nightmare of oppression. "Alister," she whispered.

"My darling, my darling."

"Save me, Alister," she continued. "Save me."

"Will you marry me to-morrow, and I shall guard and keep you always from all fear?"

"Yes, yes." She clung trembling to him. "Keep me safe, Alister. Keep me safe."

Calum and his three sons were delighted with the success of Alister's suit, and much discussion followed, and plans for the wedding on the morrow were discussed late into the night.

The ceremony was fixed for evening of the following day, and at daybreak, Calum and his sons were astir. Provisions for the wedding feast had to be obtained, guests invited, the priest fetched, and a hundred things seen to within the all too limited time available, and so it befell that, for the greater part of the day, Mary was left alone.

The sun was declining when Calum, Big Fair John, and Alister together returned. They were in high spirits, laughing and talking as they flung open the door and entered the house. A strong smell of burning immediately assailed their nostrils. The room was full of smoke ascending in volumes from the charred remains of girdle scones suspended over the fire.

"Mary," shouted Calum, much annoyed by this careless waste of food.

There was no answer.

"Mary,"—louder ; but still she did not reply. The men stared at each other. Could she possibly have wandered away alone again, forgetful of her wedding but a few hours distant, and all the necessary arrangements for that event ? Where could she be ? They

searched the house ; but no Mary was within—
the outhouses and steading ; all in vain.

" Let us look for her by the loch," counselled
Big Fair John.

They set forth accordingly and within ten
minutes came within sight of the water.
Following the course of a little burn they
therefore were themselves screened from view
by high banks on either hand. As they were
about to emerge from their concealment
Calum suddenly stopped and pointed. The
two other men looking as they were directed,
saw, to their surprise, Mary walking with a
youth who was not so far distant but that Big
Fair John could recognise him as the stranger
whom once before he had encountered with his
sister. That chance meeting had, of course,
been reported by Big Fair John to his father
and brothers who had made light of it. Certainly none had supposed that the stranger
might either linger near or return. But now
suspicions and resentment were aroused in the
minds of Mary's kinsmen and even Alister's
face flushed angrily. This intruder must be
banished once and for all.

A whispered consultation ensued, as a result
of which it was determined to take the stranger
unawares. He had not seen them : he and
Mary were walking slowly inland and would

presently pass round a knoll. Calum's plan
was to wait until the two companions had
disappeared from view and then, by running
round the eminence, to confront them so
suddenly that escape would be impossible.
A few moments later, the way being clear,
the men rushed from their hiding place and
raced to intercept the intended victim of their
wrath. But misfortune overtook them ; in
their haste they all three floundered into a
moss quagmire of peat from which they were
able to extricate themselves only after frantic
efforts. Panting and bemired they scrambled
again on their way. But this delay seemed to
have been fatal to their hopes. Warning of
their approach seemed to have been given, for
when they at length rounded the hillock, Mary
was fleeing for home, and the stranger was
nowhere to be seen. He could not, however,
have gone far, for a horse, which could belong
to no other than he, stood peacefully grazing.
They shouted to the girl, bidding her stay ;
but she only ran the faster ; and, after a few
such ineffectual efforts, they let her go ; for
their main purpose was to catch the man.

They separated, rushing hither and thither,
examining every hole and corner ; but search
as they might, nothing of the stranger was to
be seen. Perplexed and angry the men once
more met to discuss their next procedure.

Q

"Let us, at least, secure his horse," said Alister.

To that suggestion all agreed, and the young man therefore himself walked forward to capture the animal.

But when he had advanced only a few paces Calum suddenly called after him. "Stop!" he bade.

Alister paused and turned an enquiring face. "That is a strange looking beast," remarked Calum. "I have never seen the like of him."

The horse was a magnificent creature, black and glossy, with flowing mane and tail, but in two particulars its appearance was unpleasing : its head seemed to flatten slightly towards the muzzle, and the eye which it turned on them seemed to have a strangely malevolent look.

In spite of his future father-in-law's misgivings, Alister only laughed. "He is a better beast than I have ever seen," he commented. "He shall be yours from this day ; for, as he is already bridled, I shall ride him home."

Perhaps some vague recollection of his dying wife's vision was recalled, for a sudden premonition of disaster seized on Calum. "Stay! Stay!" he shouted.

But the warning was unheeded. The horse stood patiently, and Alister, folding his plaid around him, vaulted easily on the animal's back and gathered up the reins. For one moment the horse stood stock still, the next it bounded in the air, and, with a shrill, unearthly neigh, sped like lightning past Calum and his sons.

"Throw yourself off. Throw yourself off," yelled the older man in agonized tones.

And Alister, too, seemed to have caught alarm; for they heard him cry—a cry of despair—as he was borne onward. And though he struggled he seemed wholly unable to dislodge himself from the creature he bestrode, helpless to move hand or foot, as if assailed by some frightful paralysis—quicker, quicker in headlong flight.

Terror-struck the men rushed up the hillside to view that career. Straight towards the loch the horse and its rider sped until the margin was reached. With one stupendous bound they soared for a moment in the air, the next, with a mighty splash the waters rose around them, surged angrily, and then smoothed out their surface and gradually painted again the peaceful reflexion of evening sky and purple hill, unperturbed, as if no hideous secrets lay hidden beneath. The men fled to the loch-side and stood waiting, shaken to the soul by the scene which they had witnessed, hoping against hope that Alister might reappear ; but not a ripple disturbed the waters, no sign of life.

Calum's face was deadly pale, but his eyes glowed and a grim and terrible resolve seemed to set his features like a stone. " Come," he bade his son ; and so together they turned away. When they had retreated some distance he paused again. " I know now," he said, " the evil which has befallen our household. Leave me here and go home. Tell our guests, who must now have assembled, to depart as no wedding will take place there this night. Say not a word of what you have just seen, and bring your brothers here secretly, swiftly and armed."

Half an hour later the three young men joined their father and by his command all crouched with him, concealed in the bracken, about fifty yards from the shore. In whispers he told his two younger sons what he and their brother had seen. He confided to them his terrible convictions concerning the stranger who had disappeared, and he divulged his plan for the capture of this being. He urged them to be courageous and to stand by him whatever might happen, and, as they stared aghast at him, "Do not doubt," he concluded, "that what I have told you is true, and, if so he will come again from the water there in

human form, and then may the Cross of Christ
be upon us."

The sun had meanwhile set, dusk descended
and stars twinkled, palely reflected in the loch.
Great slabs of rock protruded from the shore
at this spot, on the landward side of which
reeds and rushes grew densely, giving place at
length to a stretch of smooth sward. Beyond
the rocks the blackness of the waters indicated
their extreme depth. There the horse had
leaped and less than a stone's throw distant
the men kept watch.

Hours passed and darkness deepened, no
sound broke the stillness but the gentle lap,
lap of the waters as faint winds of night ruffled
at times the surface of the loch. The waiting
men sat in silence, without moving, hidden by
the canopy of fronds around them. Midnight
came at length, and far over the dark hills the
silver light of a rising moon shone effulgently
and lit a scintillating stream of glory on the
waters. Hush! What was that? A sudden
splash! And surely there, amongst the rocks,
something was moving, something that slowly
emerged from the depth, drawing itself
upward. Young Fair John gasped and seemed
about to leap to his feet but Calum's hand
gripped his son's arm like a vice and the
trembling youth crouched silently again.
They saw the thing creeping now, creeping

upward until suddenly it stood erect in form of a man, with pale face and dark, backward-flung hair. And Calum and Big Fair John knew that the stranger whom they had seen a few hours earlier had thus returned. He stood for a few moments and seemed to listen and look around ; but, assured that he was unobserved, he presently stepped shoreward still moving awkwardly, as if lame. He reached the level turf, again looked about him, and then, flinging out his arms, he danced in the moonlight. Human though his shape was, yet something beast-like was in the uncouth contortions of his limbs, obscene, abominable. He pranced and leaped as if in exuberance of delight and then, suddenly ceasing, he flung back his head and pealed forth a long neighing laugh.

So loathsome seemed that outburst to the brothers that they had almost rushed there and then upon the creature from whom it came ; but their father imposed silence on them and so, trembling, they crouched again. They saw the stranger move off at length, making his way towards the farm. Stealthily they followed him, keeping him in sight, but careful not to disclose their presence to him. When he approached the house, not a glimmer of light was seen from any window, all was in darkness and silence, apparently deserted.

He stood for a moment as if uncertain how to proceed; then very cautiously, treading lightly, he drew nearer and, standing full in the moonlight, whistled softly.

The men who followed had kept themselves well in the shadows, still about fifty paces from the other; but now, at a signal from Calum, they stepped boldly out and advanced on the being who stood before them. Instantly he turned and seemed as if about to flee; but, perhaps realising the futility of that effort, stood quietly awaiting them.

"Whom do you seek?" demanded Calum, approaching him,

"Anyone," the stranger answered, "who will take pity on a wayfarer and afford him shelter for the night."

"Whence have you come?"

"I am a traveller from a distant land."

Big Fair John now advanced, pushing past his father and confronting the stranger with a hatred which overcame the fear within his heart. "You lie," he denounced, "as you lied to me when last we met. We have seen you . . . . ."

"Silence, fool!" thundered Calum, and thrust his son aside again. He turned to the stranger. "As you seek shelter," he said, "you are welcome to such as our poor house can afford. Enter." And he pointed the way.

The stranger hesitated ; but if he still had hopes of escape, these were obviously less than ever, for the three brothers now stood so that flight was impossible for him.

Calum strode towards the door, pushed it violently open and started back, for there stood Mary, pale as a ghost, gazing wildly from one to the other, terror-stricken.

Calum laughed. " That is well," he greeted her. " We have brought a friend of yours with us, to give him lodging for the night."

With outstretched hands, blindly, and without a word she made as if to rush past them.

But Calum caught her roughly by the wrist and swung her back again. " Not so," he forbade, "not so. We all must be present for the entertainment of our guest."

They pushed the girl and her lover (if such he were) before them, through the doorway, into the house. Though a few dying embers of peat lingered on the hearth, the room was in complete darkness ; but Calum, striking a flint, blew a tinder to a flame and lighted a rush-light which dimly illumined the scene— the four hulking kinsmen, the shrinking girl, the tall stranger from whose pale face the eyes glittered like coals of fire, and the distorted shadows of all which leaped on roof and walls. Calum held the light for a moment above the stranger's head and saw, as he had expected, green water-weeds intermingled with the long black hair of the terrible being. Shuddering, but without a word he turned towards Mary. "Go kindle a fire," he bade her. "There is a marriage feast which we shall share to-night, though the bridegroom is late." He again faced the stranger. "Have you seen anything of him?" he asked.

"How should I know him," answered the other, "though I were to meet him?"

"True," Calum answered, "but we know him as a friend so faithful and so dear that any wrong to him we would avenge to the last drop of our blood. Meanwhile, will you be seated?"

"Thank you," answered the stranger, and with complete composure laid hold of a chair and prepared to sit on it.

But Calum suddenly wrenched it violently away.

"Not on that," he forbade. "That is not worthy of an honoured guest." He pointed to a bed. "There," he directed, "you will find that more comfortable."

The stranger sat where he was bidden, and at once Big Fair John and Middle Fair John, the most stalwart of the brothers, sat also, one on either side of him. Hardly, however, had they

taken their places when the young men, at a
signal from their father, locked their arms
around the stranger and threw him backward
on the bed. With a shout Calum and his
youngest son sprang to the assistance of the
others and instantly a scene of the wildest
confusion followed. Though four gigantic
Highlanders wrestled with him, the stranger
seemed to be possessed with superhuman
power and dragged them all to the floor. The
table was overturned, extinguishing the light
and plunging the room again in darkness. With
a piercing scream, Mary, who had been kneeling
on the hearth, arose and fled from the house
into the night. Then came a terror which
had nearly driven the reason from the minds of
father and sons, of which afterwards they
spoke only in whispers ; for beneath their
hands they felt the form with which they
grappled suddenly expand until it was no
longer human, but that of a huge beast—a
horse which flung them from it, plunging,
trampling in that confined space. For a
moment panic seized them and they shrank
appalled. Then, "In God's Name !" shouted
Calum, and, dirk in hand, he fell once more
upon the monster. Inspired by their father's
indomitable courage the sons, too, renewed
their attack. They were kicked and flung
hither and thither, but they rushed in again.

They hacked, they stabbed with their dirks, while the thing they fought screamed in shrill, unearthly clamour. It fell upon the floor and writhed in awful convulsions ; but they showed no mercy. It quivered at length, stretched its limbs, and lay dead.

All but dead, too, were the four men who staggered from the house, and, supporting, half dragging each other, fled from the defilement of that lifeless thing they had left behind. Only when some hundreds of yards had been covered did they fall prone and speechless on the heather, there to lie until the dawn renewed their strength.

Painfully Calum arose. "Come," he bade , "that which we have left behind cannot remain there. We must carry it out or else burn the house about it."

The gray light of morning broke coldly on them as father and sons paused outside their dwelling. They listened—not a sign of life, no sound disturbed the complete silence. The door stood ajar. Suddenly bursting it open, Calum, followed by his sons rushed within— nothing, no carcase lay there. And yet, what was that on the floor ? They stooped, gazed and recoiled in abhorrence and disgust ; for before them was a heap of slime only, gelatinous, foul and smelling of corruption. No choice now but to fire the house unfit for further human habitation. So they stood and watched the flames lick up the rafters, and crackle in the thatch, watched until that which once had been their home was a roaring furnace of flames. Then they turned about and departed.

One thing remained to be done—Mary must be found. But their search was not long; they saw her lying, apparently lifeless, in the heather near the loch. If resentment towards her had lingered in their thoughts, that was now dispelled—pale, hardly breathing as she was, yet she opened her eyes as they bent over her. Very gently they raised her to her feet.

She looked around her, as if searching for someone. Suddenly she pointed towards the loch. "Alister," she whispered.

Startled, they turned to gaze in the direction indicated. But it was not Alister they saw—only his plaid floating on the surface of the water, close to a shelving shore. With a cry Mary started to run towards the spot.

Then it was that Calum recalled clearly his dying wife's vision, and he knew that none should look on what these dark waters had yielded up. "Stop!" he cried, and tried to hold his daughter.

But she eluded him and sped on. They overtook her only when the shore had been reached. Perhaps the plaid had been caught by some spur of rock from which it had only recently fallen; for it floated as the ripples toyed idly with it, above the pebbles, And there beneath it, undulated by the water, lay an unspeakable horror, mangled, half-devoured, rent from that which once had been a man.

Mary saw it, gazed a moment with dilated eyes, and then, uttering shriek upon shriek, she fled to the hills, distraught in that insanity from which she was destined never to recover.

AN ECHO FROM THE PAST.

Cha d' dhùin dorus nach d'fhosgail dorus.
No door closes without opening another door.

AN unclouded sky ; billowing Highland hills, bracken and heather clad, glistening with moisture from innumerable springs ; soft shadows lingering in deep valleys through which tumbled tempestuously burns of amber-clear waters flecked with foam ; clusters of stunted oak trees, birch, and hazel, lichened, age-old remnants of forest which formerly had clothed the landscape ; the plaintive cry of curlew circling above, the chuckle of grouse, the far bleat of sheep, the solitude and peace which reigned supreme, all called and beckoned me to leave my friends and the car by which they would complete their journey, and to strike out on foot and alone over the hills to the inn which was intended as our resting-place that night.

The map over which I pored seemed to prove clearly that by taking the direct road— a cart track—I should avoid a long detour followed by the highway. Indeed, there seemed no reason why—unless fortune failed me—I should not reach our destination almost as soon as my less energetic friends. In that exhilarating mountain air what was a walk of nine or ten miles to me ?

I set off, accordingly, so assured by the blue sky and sunshine that coat and waterproof were left behind ; my only burden was a stout ash walking-stick.

"Don't get lost amongst the hills," shouted one of my friends in warning as I trudged off.

Ridiculous suggestion ! Were it winter and amidst snow-drifts some such risk there might have been ; but with the long evening of early autumn before me, an untroubled sky over-head, and a path so clearly traced upon the map, what was there to fear ?

For an hour I climbed by the side of a burn, my way leading without ever a turn, so that, looking back, I could see the house from which I had set out—the car still standing by the door. I should certainly outstrip my friends and reach our next resting-place without my luggage conveyed by them. Still upward and onward, and a wonderful panorama was un-folded before me : hills beyond hills melting into the blue horizon, valleys cleft by rushing streams which through ages had chiselled the rocks and wrought from them fairy-like grottos and cascades all hung about with drooping mountain-ash and hazel trees, with fern and heather wet by ever-ascending clouds of spray.

Beguiled by the beauty of one of these ravines, and breathless from my long climb, I stepped aside and sat by the water. High banks rose on either hand, and so steeply as to shut out all but a narrow strip of sky. Lulled by the sound of the rushing burn, and cushioned by a deep heather bed, I lingered drowsily for longer than I had purposed. Quite half an hour must have passed before I shivered, conscious of a chill breath of wind stealing up the glen, and that the sunshine had given place to gloom. I hurriedly regained the track and found that meanwhile the sky had become overcast with clouds, and that angry gusts of wind blew from the southwest. The change had come with amazing rapidity. In place of sun-steeped hills, smiling in seeming sleep, I saw frowning heights which gloomily withdrew behind thick cloaks of drifting mist. A fine drizzle of rain, too, dewed my clothing and wet my cheek. I had been foolish to linger so long by the burn. I must hurry on and make up if possible for lost time.

Sometimes skirting the shoulders of hills, at others following the course of long valleys, I tramped on until the track, gradually ascending, led me steeply upward. The mist by this time had gathered more densely, descending on the hilltops, and heavy rain fell. Every step led me farther into the cloud and saturated my feet and legs from the dripping heather and bracken through which I plunged. Still, there must now be no turning back having already progressed so far. Another hour or so would see me at my journey's end. I noticed with annoyance and a little anxiety that the track showed very uncertainly—had dwindled indeed to little more than a sheep path. Confident, however, that I had not lost my way, I dismissed all fear and trudged on.

Thicker and ever thicker grew the mist around me. I could hardly see ten yards ahead. The hillside was now broken into deep clefts and seams where the peat of its surface had been burst asunder by alternate frosts and heat, or worn away by tiny trickles from the many streams and rain. These had collected in the indentations, forming pools clear but amber-coloured, or coarse and vividly green moss overlaid treacherous mire of mingled peat and water. Level reaches afforded no ease to the climber, for these were invariably moss-grown morasses in which a footfall might have plunged the unwary inextricably. Great boulders strewed the slopes and loomed ghostly through the obscured atmosphere. Indeed, so uneven and broken was the surface of the ground that after a time I had to face the fact that I had lost the track. To make matters worse, the rain was now descending in torrents and the mist enveloped me in drifting clouds.

Thoroughly alarmed by my situation, I

R

stumbled panting, determined that night should not overtake me as a wanderer. Sometimes I slid on the edge on the deep crevasses and before I could recover my foothold had plunged knee-deep in the mire which they harboured. On hands and knees I had often to extricate myself from the trap into which I had fallen. I was soon, of course, soaked to the skin, and plastered from head to heel with peat. No living being was to be seen save that from time to time a blue mountain hare started from the dripping bracken and, showering the moisture about it, fled from my approach; or, with startled outcry, grouse took wing and vanished into the mist.

I knew how easily those lost in such circumstances as mine may wander in a circle, and I determined, therefore, to follow the next decline, reach a burn, and pursue its course in the hope of finding a sheep farm or shepherd's cottage where I might seek direction on my way. But I found my quest not so easy as I had supposed, though to my unobstructed view the whole range of hills had seemed interwoven by streams. Another hour passed before, to my joy, I heard the clamour of a waterfall, and presently found myself by the banks of a burn.

By this time I was thoroughly exhausted and forced to rest, despite the fact that daylight was fading fast. Dusk, indeed, had fallen when, half an hour after, I rose and plodded onward. A catastrophe which all but deprived me of my last hope of reaching shelter that night overtook me when, floundering over fern-concealed rocks, I strained an ankle. The pain was so severe that I had to bind up the injured joint with a handkerchief torn into strips before proceeding haltingly and in darkness.

By the light of a match my watch pointed to nine o'clock—four and a half hours since I had set out. Very soon the lights in farmhouses and cottages would be extinguished, so that, even should I approach one of these, without a guiding ray I might easily pass by. My progress, too, was very slow over the rough bank of the burn into which I had no mind to fall. Meeting at length a stone dyke which seemed to offer a miserable sort of shelter, I determined that there must be my halting-place until daylight, but that before this surrender I should climb the steep bank to a height from which I might look out for any sign of habitation. By the dyke side I dragged my weary self upward from the water level without much hope of success in my search, reached a gate and saw to my inexpressible joy, not fifty yards distant, a broad beam of light from a cottage window.

I had almost shouted in my relief, and stumbling forward in eager haste, found myself brought up sprawling on a barbed-wire fence from which I extricated myself only after much damage to my clothing. With greater caution I crawled beneath the unarmed wires of the abominable obstacle and reached the little house. It was obviously that of a shepherd—two-roomed as far as I could judge at the moment, and thatched. A cow-house stood near. A poverty-stricken attempt at a garden stretched before, and behind all, rose a cluster of tall trees, their dark foliage just discernible against the sky.

My footsteps aroused a furious clamour from a dog within, an uproar redoubled as I knocked and waited an answer to my summons. The window-blind had been drawn so that I could not see from whom I was about to ask for succour. I heard steps approaching. A low voice bade the dog be silent, a command which was complainingly obeyed. A bolt was withdrawn and the door flung boldly open.

No figure of romance confronted me but that of a buxom and pleasantly featured woman who stood holding high a lighted candle, and peering out into the night, while from behind her skirts protruded the watchful and snarling face of a collie.

I must have presented a terrifying appearance, bemired from head to heel, soaked to the skin and with tattered raiment ; but not a trace of fear was to be seen in the face of the good wife. She gazed in astonishment indeed.

" Who will you be seekin' ? " she asked sharply.

I stepped forward, to the further displeasure of the collie, which growled savagely. A backward swing of its mistress's foot, however, again silenced the brute.

" I am very sorry to disturb you at so late an hour," I said ; " but the fact is that I have lost my way amongst the hills, and seeing the light of your window I have come to ask if you can direct me. What is the name of this house ? "

" It's called Glenoran," she answered ; " and where would you be meaning to go ? "

I told her of the inn which I had hoped to reach ere nightfall, of my friends left behind, and of my own rash attempt to find my way on foot.

" Oh ! " she exclaimed. " You will have made a long round. You're six miles or more away." She mentioned the name of the inn.

" Six miles ! " She might as well have said sixty as far as my inclination to cover the distance in my present plight was concerned. " Are you the wife of a shepherd ? " I asked.

" Aye."

" Perhaps you and your husband will allow

me to rest here for a while. You see," I gestured, " I am in rather a sorry state."

" My man's awa' wi' a flock to Oban an' he'll no be back till to-morrow night, may be."

" In that case, of course, I must not trespass on your hospitality," I said, though with a sinking heart.

" What for no ? " she queried. " Will you no come ben and rest yoursel ? "

I thankfully accepted the invitation, and followed my hostess into what was apparently the principal room of the cottage. A great peat fire smouldered on the hearth and diffused a pungent odour. A rag mat covered the hearth, and in the warm glow three rotund and woolly pups huddled together—the family of the collie which still slunk at the woman's heels and continued to keep a watchful eye on me. Two wooden armchairs with red cushions were placed on either side of the room, and by the wall opposite the window stood a box bed. All was scrupulously clean and neat, and presented a picture of comfort very alluring to me in my wretched fatigue.

My hostess—Mrs. MacKenzie she told me was her name—eyeing me in the light of a lamp which burned on the table, was evidently aghast at my condition. The chill of her reticence melted to the warmth of kindly hospitality as she bade me be seated and insisted that I must eat, spreading a snowy tablecloth, preparing tea, boiled eggs, great fleecy scones and butter for my refreshment. Never had food and drink been more acceptable to me. The glowing hearth, the song of the steaming kettle, the warmth of the cheerful room, and the simple-hearted kindness of the woman who welcomed me to a share in these, was to me sheer delight. Without the least trace of self-consciousness this peasant had the instincts of the true gentlewoman— quiet dignity, no effort to appear otherwise than as Providence had designed. Herself respecting her place in life, she commanded respect from others. Shrewd and sensible, too, she was, and not without the sense of humour—a type of the Highland hill-dweller, one of the finest races in the world.

She told me that her " good man would be real vexed to have missed me ; " they lived a very solitary life two miles or more distant from the farm and far removed from all other dwellings. The opportunities which they had, accordingly, for a ' crack ' with a stranger were few and far between. Was she frightened to be left alone ? " Frightened ? What was there to fear. It was'na as if she had any gear to tempt a thief. They were honest folk in the hills. Besides, she and ' Glen ' (the collie) were weel able to fend for themsels,"

At length I arose to take a limping departure. The hour was late. I had already, I knew, far outstayed the usual bedtime of the cottagers in these parts.

But the kindly soul indignantly combated my intention to set forth. I " wasna able to travel wi' a sair fit and on sic a like night. What wud her good man say if he kenned she had turned a gentleman like me fra the door? Hoot, the idea was fair rediculous. Trouble! There'd be nae trouble. She would occupy the adjoining room and I was welcome to the bed there ; to be sure, it would be mair homely-like than I was used to."

I confess that I was glad to have my scruples overborne. I really was unfit to walk another six weary miles, even should the prospects of finding my way in the dark have been less hopeless than they were. Rightly or wrongly I agreed to stay.

Mrs. MacKenzie heaped more peat upon the fire, charged me to hang my wet clothes before the blaze, relighted her extinguished candle, bade me good-night and withdrew. Barely three minutes later, however, she tapped on the door and, with the only signs of embarrassment I ever saw her display, thrust into my grasp a red flannel night-shirt, evidently the property of her husband.

For perhaps an hour I sat before the fire

listening to the drip of the rain upon the thatch without, to the loud tumult of the burn's swollen waters as they leaped from pool to pool and poured thunderously over a fall at no great distance from the house. The collie and her family were coiled together contentedly and asleep at my feet on the hearth.

I am certain that I did not sleep. I remember quite clearly that sitting there my thoughts had wandered to my friends. I wondered whether my absence had greatly alarmed them ; if at the moment they were searching the hills for me. So concerned was I at the needless anxiety which in all probability I had aroused, so plunged was I in these reflections, that I started, conscious at length of commotion which for some time had continued without : voices in angry altercation, shouts and cries. I had heard them approach ; but so preoccupied had I been that I had paid no heed. Now they forced themselves on my notice—not to be ignored. Men were out there, close at hand, a crowd of men, in excitement or anger or both. Who could they be ? Perhaps the husband of my hostess and with him drunken companions with whom he had quarrelled. He would be surprised to find me there. Would he resent my presence in spite of his wife's assurances to the contrary ? I might find difficulty in dealing with him if he were drunk. Strange that his wife had not hurried to unbolt the door and let him in. I would forestall her. Even the collie was disturbed ; she sat up with pricked ears, listening, growling, and followed at my heels as I hurried from the room, groped in the darkened passage and at length threw open the outer door. Something brushed my legs. Glancing round, I saw the collie sneaking back into the kitchen, her tail between her legs. Without— nothing but the black night, mist and rain drifting on my face ; only the roar of the burn. Yet I felt certain that I had not been deceived. There had been men close at hand but a few moments before. Why now were they silent ? " Who is there ? " I called. No answer came. Very strange ! But I would investigate no further. Perhaps, after all, I had been mistaken. I closed and bolted the door softly and turned to re-enter the room. I noticed the dog standing on the hearth with bristling back and bared fangs ; but as I advanced she seemed pacified and soon flung herself again by her puppies. Mrs. MacKenzie in the adjoining room had made no sign or movement.

Intolerably tired and sleepy, I determined to go to bed. I was accordingly soon arrayed in the flannel night-shirt and between the sheets, the table with the extinguished lamp and a box of matches within easy reach. Flames still leaped from the peat on the fire, and cast wayward shadows on walls and ceiling. Watching these I fell asleep.

Dreams, disturbing, terrifying dreams ! Clamour intermingled with menacing, guttural snarls ! I started up bewildered, forgetful for the moment where I was until the room, dimly seen by the still flickering light of the fire, recalled the memory of these. I heard sounds of wild disturbance ; but through these and closer at hand the savage threatening of the collie's growl, rising, falling with every intake and expiration of her breath. I could see her crouching but with head turned towards the window, afraid yet dangerous. But the brute claimed my attention no longer than a moment. The sounds from without were those which startled me ; for again I heard clearly the shouting of men's voices. The rushing of the burn of course dominated all other noises ; but distinctly through the uproar of the waters I heard wild human cries and groans. Anger, excitement, triumph, despair—all seemed to be expressed.

Then—I confess—I felt afraid. Fear shook me, sent icy shivers down my back. Some deed of horrible violence was surely being perpetrated close at hand, mysteriously, under cover of darkness and by a great concourse of men. I had not previously been deceived. They had been there when I looked out. But alone though I had been, they had shunned detection by me and hidden themselves. Now, become bolder or carried away by excitement, they had broken again into their appalling tumult.

Curiosity mastered fear. I felt that at all costs I must know the explanation of this uproar. And so, shaking though I was, I scrambled from the bed to the floor. Trivial though it may seem, the sight of my ridiculous red flannel night-shirt arrested me. It was short, too, and would therefore doubly render me the butt of jest and the victim of the storm. I could not face a crowd of men or even the solitary Mrs. MacKenzie in that garment. I must reclothe myself; but for a moment I hesitated. All this while, you must understand, the collie had stood snarling. Just for a second as I climbed to the floor she had turned her head towards me; then she crouched, watchful again of the window.

Quite suddenly a sound arose which seemed to contract every pulse within me, and drew from the animal with upturned face a long, shuddering, whimper of misery or terror, I knew not which—a woman's shriek. It pierced through all other clamour of voices and of waters; it stabbed through the night to my very heart, so agonized, so despairing was it. For a few moments it seemed to have been muffled as by a cloak drawn over the mouth; then it broke forth again more shrill, more horrifying than before.

I could hesitate no longer with that appeal ringing in my ears. I shouted incoherently. I flung myself on my boots and clothing and wrenched them on anyhow. Every nerve in my body quivered in my frantic haste. Still these piercing cries arose, but more distantly. Of what horror of cruelty was this woman the victim? I could not bear it. She was being borne away, or maddened trying to rush from her tormentors. Stumbling, panting, I fled from the room, tore open the outer door and with outspread hands before me leaped into the night, tripped, and fell headlong on the garden path. Up again I stood listening— not a sound but that of the burn tumbling, churning its rocky and precipitous bed.

I was utterly dumbfounded. Was I mad? Or the victim of a stupendous hoax? It was inconceivable that all the turmoil, shouts, and cries which I had so clearly heard should cease on the moment. Yet, not a whisper left. Only the splash of the hurrying stream and the deeper rumble of the waterfall.

A glimmer of light caught my eyes and I

turned to see the window of Mrs. MacKenzie's room flickeringly illuminated. She, too, must have been disturbed and was evidently lighting a candle. As I groped my way towards the cottage entrance my hostess's door opened slightly and her head, with plaited hair hanging on either side, was thrust through the aperture. Her eyes were round with amazement or fear.

" What ails ye ? " she asked sharply.

" What is the meaning of this uproar ? " I counter queried. " It is impossible that you cannot have heard—the shouting—the cries—the woman's screams. There has been some horrible violence. People are there in hiding —crowds of them. I don't want to alarm you ; but you must explain it if you can. Something must be done. What does it mean ? "

She eyed me steadily. " That beats a'," she said.

I sprang towards her. " Don't you understand ? " I cried. " I tell you that there has been some terrible outrage perpetrated : I heard a woman screaming for help. You must have heard."

" You've been dreamin'," she answered me, and added as I stood speechless : " but it's very queer for a' that."

" Do you mean to tell me that you have heard nothing ? "

" There's nothin' to hear but the burn. You can just gang back to bed. Na, na ; there's nothin' to fear. I'm real sorry you have heard the sounds though. I thought my good-man was the only one."

" Your husband, too, has heard before now these cries ? " I asked.

" Many's the time he's thought so ; but aye when he's been a wee thing out o' sorts like, you ken. There's no cries whatever. Gang back to bed. I'll warrant you'll hear no more cries the night. But I'm very distressed you have been feared, for a' that."

The simple sincerity of the woman was not to be doubted ; and it left me abashed, bewildered, questioning the evidences of my own senses. I slunk off to my bed in the kitchen, there to lie sleepless until the grey light of dawn was stealing through the window.

I was awakened at an early hour by Mrs. Mackenzie, who beat upon the door and told me that while she milked the cow I could wash and dress in the room just vacated by her. About an hour later I breakfasted with her on steaming porridge and new-laid eggs.

Fortified by these refreshments and with morning sunshine streaming on us I was better prepared than in the night to accept her assurances. I must have been betrayed by my imagination. We were miles from all other dwellings. No trace was without of footsteps other than my own. No one, saving myself, had approached the house during the night. I may have been feverish and the sounds I seemed to have heard, only those of delirious creation. Perhaps the roar of the burn had deceived me.

Strange, however, that, as she again told me, this woman's husband should have been alarmed repeatedly by the same delusions. Often he had started up awakened from sleep convinced that he heard shouts and cries from without. His " daft dreams " she called them. I should like to have met that man and compared notes with him ; but I have never had the chance. Very strange, too, and inexplicable, had been the behaviour of the dog.

I tried, however, to make light of the matter at the moment, apologized deeply for having needlessly aroused my kind hostess from her slumbers, thanked her again and again for her hospitality (for which she indignantly refused all payment) and was escorted by her to the door.

I looked with considerable curiosity on the scene of the imaginings of the previous night, now rain-washed and glistening in the sunshine. Red and foam-flecked the burn plunged not twenty yards beneath. Farther up its course, and embowered by mountain ash

trees, the waterfall thundered, its spray drifting, rainbow-tinted. High on the farther
bank stood a crumbling ruin all hung about
with ivy—the remains apparently of one of the
Highland strongholds. Mounds of earth, with
broken masonry interspersed, showed where its
once massive outer defences and walls had
stood.

"That's a fine old ruin," I remarked to Mrs.
MacKenzie. "Aye," she answered, "that's
Glenoran Castle. You will have heard of it."

"No, I could not recall the name."

"Awell, there's a good many folk that whiles
comes to see it. Your way is doon the burn
until you come to the sheep road, and that'll
lead the way you would be going."

And so I bade farewell to Glenoran and the
kindly shepherd's wife, nor have I ever had an
opportunity of renewing acquaintance with
either, though neither could I ever forget.

"Glenoran!" exclaimed one of my friends
after I had rejoined them, but without having
told of my midnight adventures. "A most
interesting place and well worth a visit. You
know its story, of course. No? Oh, well,
you must read the ballad for yourself. The
castle was owned by a great chief who was
treacherously taken by Argyll and hanged by
night before the castle walls. The man's
wife is said to have pleaded in vain for his life,

s

and in the madness of her grief to have rushed to a waterfall near by that its noise might drown the shouts which announced her husband's execution. The place is named the Lynn of Sorrow to this day. A legend which is quite probably unhistorical.

I happened, however, to know that the story was true; for if ever the restless and complaining spirits of the dead can linger on earth, that place is so haunted; or it may be that human agony so permeates even material objects in the scene of suffering, that these for ever after reverberate and echo anguish to the ear atuned to hear.

APPENDICES.

THE BLACK DOG OF MACPHIE.

THIS story, several versions of which are extant, illustrates the belief in fairy women, their enmity to the hunter, their beauty and powers of enchanting men and their aversion from dogs. The tale as told in this book follows fairly closely, though in much extended form, one of the versions given by Mr. Campbell in his *Superstitions of the Scottish Highlands*. The conclusion, as here related, is without authority. The true rendering as given by Mr Campbell is as follows:—" When the light of day appeared Macphie looked and he had not a single man alive of those who were with him in the cave. He took with him the hand and went to the shore to the boat. He went on board and went to Colonsay, unaccompanied by dog or man. He took the hand up with him that men might see the horror he had met with, the night he was in the cave. No man in Islay or Colonsay ever at all saw such a hand, nor did they imagine that such existed."

It will thus be seen that I have taken the liberty (perhaps unpardonably) of introducing the incident of the hand being whistled back by its unseen owner.

One wonders whether in this old Highland legend Guy de Maupassant found material for his famous story, " The Hand."

THYRA.

THE story of Thyra as told by Mr. Campbell is brief, but may be further slightly abridged as follows :—
"At one time the King of Denmark is said to have sent his son to the Scottish Court along with six others. They landed in Caithness where, as they came chiefly for sport, they began to look for deer and other wild animals and to inquire where they were to be found. They were told that all animals of the chase had become scarce since more people had come to that part, but in the neighbouring parts of the country, especially in Ross-shire, they were still numerous, and if they went there they would get abundant sport. They went and while they remained, lived in a house of the MacKenzies near Loch Maree. One day when following deer on the hills the young prince got separated from his companions. Being fatigued, he sat down by the wayside and fell asleep. He was awakened by the sound of voices and on looking he saw two men, one of whom was young and the other old, coming on the road towards him with a young woman walking between. He got up and as they came nearer he was making out that he never saw a more beautiful woman. The old man said, " You are doing wrong in delaying us on our way." " Me-thinks," said the prince, " that I am not doing any-thing out of the way, nor have I spoken a wrong

word." The old man got angry and called him rough names and said he was ill-bred. "That was not the way in which I was taught," the prince answered. "I have the blood of the Kings of Denmark in my veins and I am inclined to put your head as low as your shoes for your ill words which I have not deserved." When the old man heard this he became afraid and made excuses for the warmth of temper he had shown, but said he was bound to protect the girl, as she herself was under vows of the Church by her father's commands. He added that they had come ashore from the monastery of Isle Maree and must return thither before nightfall. The prince demanded to be told the maiden's name. "Her name," the old man answered, "is Princess Thyra of the house of Ulster in Ireland. In parting the prince said to the maiden, "As this has been our first meeting, so I fear is it to be our last. Farewell!" "I do not say," she answered. He went home, returning to the same spot the next day, hoping to meet the maiden, but in vain. Day after day he returned without success until three days had passed and he was ill pleased at his mischance. He was told that a man on the other side of the loch had a boat, so he went to him and got him to go with him. On landing the man pointed out to him the way to the monastery and told him that he would come to a well which he was not to pass till he drank of its water which was efficacious in every malady to which mankind is subject. Beside the well was a tree with a hollow in its side in which all wayfarers were expected to put something of value. The prince pursued his way, but forgot the well and the tree. Having reached the house he demanded admittance and that he might see the Irish princess. But his request was refused. "If I want her for my wife and she consents, can you prevent the union?" he then asked. "We will leave the matter to her own will," the old monk answered. She came gladly and the prince spent that day on the isle. Before he left she said, "I have a doubt in this matter." "What is that?" he asked. "It is that I never saw you but once before now, neither did you see me, and if love comes quickly it may go as quickly." "You know that from yourself," he said. "No," she answered. He told her to look at the evening star. "As truly as that star shines on yonder hill, so truly do I love you," he vowed. "I have another doubt," she said. "Your doubts are very many," he replied. She told him that there was one named "Red Hector of the Hills" who would be dangerous if he were to be met. The prince took his leave and having cause, as he thought, to be pleased with events, was going on joyously whistling, when an arrow passed close to his face and next instant another transfixed his bonnet. He stood looking about him and saw a big man standing beside a rock on the roadside. "What sort of a man are you, when you are going to make a target of me?" the prince asked. "Have you never heard of Red Hector of the Hills?" the other answered. " If you have not, you now see him and will feel his skill. There is a matter to settle between us which can never be done but in one way, and that is that you kill me or I kill you." They therefore took their swords, but before they fell to the prince asked if there was no other way of settling the matter but by bloodshed. " There is no other way," answered Red Hector, and struck the prince on the side, wounding him. The prince fell and Hector fled. The prince was in great agony and like to bleed to death ; so, clasping his wound with his hand, he crawled to where a little stream trickled, but before he could drink he fainted and lay unconscious there all that night and next day until the monks from the monastery found him. They took him home and he lay senseless for many weeks during which his own men who had been brought to the isle and the princess nursed him. He then told her every day how he would take her to Denmark. One day a ship was seen coming and a message was conveyed to the princess that her father lay dying. " Will you return ? " asked the prince. " I will return," she promised. " You will not forget me among your own people ? " " Nothing but death will prevent my return," she vowed.

One day the prince met an old man whom his men bade stand aside. " Do not speak so gruffly," the old man said. " I have come to you as I am in need of shelter and to ask you if you will take me into your service while you are here." " My burden is on others," the prince answered, " and little an old man like you with a staff in his hand can do to help me. Have you a house and home ? " " I had until yesterday," the old man told him, " but to-day I have nothing. I had house, wife, son, land, cattle, and yesterday every beast that I had was lifted, except a stray sheep, and my son went in search of it and fell over the rocks and was killed. When his mother heard what had happened to him she leapt into the sea and was drowned. Now I am left alone. If you will take me with you I will do you more service in the hills than a younger man can do. My name is Duighall," he added.

The prince took the old man into his service. And when one day the ship was seen conveying back the princess, he led the old man with him to the highest summit of the hills to watch. " Delay," said the old man, " till I tell you my dream." " I care nought for dreams," said the prince. " But listen, for I dreamed the same dream three nights one after the other, and it was that she was dead. " We wish joyous news and you have given us instead news of sorrow." " I will go to the ship," the old man insisted, " and when I reach it, if all is well, you will see a red signal, but if sorrow awaits you, the signal will be black." He went and found the princess. She asked if all were well. He told her that all was well, but that the prince was impatient for news. He then persuaded the princess against her will and the advice of those with her to show the death-signal, saying that the joy of seeing her living would compensate her lover for the deception.

When the signal was seen by those on land, the prince said he could no longer live and took his dagger from its sheath and killed himself. When the princess reached the shore, those who met her told her what had been done. She asked where he was and vowed that no power seen or unseen would prevent her from taking a last farewell, and that she would go alone and do no injury to herself. When she came to where his body lay, she noticed that someone was following her, and turning found that the intruder was the old man. "Wretched Duighall!" she exclaimed, "what evil advice you gave me!" "That is not my name," he declared. "I am Red Hector of the Hills and this is my revenge." He then killed her with his dirk and fled and was never seen or heard of in the country afterwards."

EWEN AND HIS SEAL WIFE.

THROUGHOUT the Western Highlands seals were believed to be, either king's children under enchantment, or fallen angels. Under the former category they were supposed to be able, on occasion, to doff their disguise and reappear in human form.

In Mr. Campbell's *Superstitions of the Scottish Highlands* a legend concerning the seals is thus told :—" There is a sept in North Uist known as " the MacCodrums of the seals " from being said to be descendants of these enchanted seals. The progenitor of the family, being down about the shore, saw the seals putting off their coverings and washing themselves. He fled home with one of the skins and hid it above the lintel of the door. . . . . The owner of the covering followed him. He clad her with human garments, married her and had a family by her. She managed ultimately to regain possession of her lost covering and disappeared."

Mrs. Kennedy Fraser has done much for the discovery and preservation of the old, so called, " sealsongs and music " of the Hebrides. That these animals can and do utter musical cries is a well authenticated fact which no doubt led to the legendary music attributed to them.

DONALD GORM.

SOME of the incidents described in this story have
been suggested by facts mentioned in the histories
of the families of MacLeod of Dunvegan and Mac-
Donald of Sleat. Donald Gorm of Sleat was the
brother-in-law of the then chief of MacLeod by
whom he was held in mortal hatred not only because
MacDonald had repudiated his marriage, but had
killed MacLeod's father. It is a historical fact that
Donald Gorm was driven by storm to seek shelter
in the castle of his enemy and tradition relates how
there he struck his dirk in the board, boastfully
confessing that there stood the knife that had killed
the father of his host and that his own hand was the
best in all the Western Highlands in the use of that
weapon. Another version of the feud is given in
Gregory's *History of the Western Highlands and
Isles*, in which mention is made of, " Trouble in the
Isles betwixt the Clan Donald and the Seil Tormot,
the year 1601," and is to the effect that the dispute
was carried on by Sir Rory MacLeod of the Herries
and Donald Gorm MacDonald of Sleat. In reference to
the incident concerning the dagger, a Gaelic song was
made of which Mr. Campbell in his *Clan Traditions
and Popular Tales* gives a translation as follows :—

" This is the dirk that killed your father,
 And it has not refused you yet,
 Farewell to you from the side of the channel."

Regarding the setting fire to the barn where the men were supposed to be asleep, in the frustrated effort to assassinate them, the present venerable Chief of MacLeod* informs me that no such order was issued by his ancestor, but that an attempt such as that described was made, without their chief's authority, by his men.

The mention of the Spirit of the Storm is an attempt to reintroduce something of the Ossianic mythology.

The death of the two principal characters of my story finds no parallel in the histories of the families to whom reference is made.

* Since deceased

THE BLACK RAVEN OF GLENGARRY.

THE direct line of the MacDonells of Glengarry is, alas, extinct; but the ruins of their old castle of Invergarry still stand on the shore of Loch Oich.

In Mr. George Eyre-Todd's *The Highland Clans of Scotland*, the following reference is made to the family :—" Of the noble old race the history is romantic in the extreme. Like the other two great branches of the Clan, the MacDonalds of the Isles and of Clanranold, which contest with Glengarry the supreme chiefship of the name, the MacDonells are directly descended from Reginald, the younger son of the famous Somerled, King of the Isles in the twelfth century. Their patronymic of MacDonald they took from Donald, the elder of Reginald's two sons. A common ancestor of all three houses was Donald's grandson, Angus Og, who supported King Robert the Bruce in the Wars of Succession, entertained him in his castle of Dunavertie in the south end of Kintyre, when he was fleeing for safety to the Island of Rachryn. . . . . . A privilege claimed by all the MacDonalds in common was the right to the post of honour on the right in all Scottish armies in the day of battle. This right was, it is said, conferred upon them by King Robert the Bruce in recognition of the part they played on the field of Bannockburn, and the ignoring of it, they declare, brought about the disastrous issue of the battles of Harlaw and Culloden."

MACEUAR.

In Mr. Campbell's *Clan Traditions and Popular Tales* the story of MacEuar (Mac-an-Uidhir) is thus related :—" The person of whom the following story is told, lived at Hynish in the island of Tiree, and had become engaged to a young woman in the neighbourhood. Between the espousal and the marriage, the young couple went with a party of friends for a sail to Heisker, near Canna. The men of the party went ashore seal-hunting, and one of the young woman's disappointed suitors took advantage of the opportunity to get Mac-an-Uidhir left behind, and, coming back to the boat, told that the intending bridegroom had been drowned. By this lie he hoped to make the bride despair of seeing her intended any more, and by renewing his own attentions to get her to consent to accept himself. She, however, not believing that he was dead, said that she would marry no one for a year and a day from the date of his alleged drowning. . . . The abandoned and castaway youth subsisted on birds and fish eaten raw for three quarters of a year, but at last got away from the island and made his way home. He arrived on the night on which the marriage of his intended to his unscrupulous rival was to take place. He went to the house of his foster-mother who did not know him, his appearance through his privations having

become so much changed, and he having asked to
remain for the night, she said she was alone and could
not let a stranger like him stay. She also told of
the festivities in the neighbourhood and said that
he had better pass the night there. He asked the
occasion of the festivities and she told him how her
foster-son had been drowned and supplanted and
that this was the night of his rival's marriage.
He then asked her if she did not recognise him and
told her who he was, but she refused to believe him.
He put the matter out of question by asking if she
would know her own handiwork and showing her
what was left of the hose she had given him, to con-
vince her. When she saw the labour of her own
hands she welcomed him and went with him where
the marriage party were. Those who were there
were surprised to see her arrival, knowing the sad
state she was in at this time of year, through the loss
of her foster-child. They, however, received the
stranger as well as herself with the utmost kindness.
The bride made the remark, when the stranger turned
his back, that he was like Mac-an-Uidhir, but when
his face was turned towards her he appeared like a
stranger whom she had never seen before, but that
her heart warmed towards him. The custom was
then gone through of the stranger drinking out of
the bride's glass, and Mac-an-Uidhir when doing
this slipped a ring into the glass, which she immediately recognised as that of her lost lover. The whole
matter was then upset, and the party for whom the

T

preparations were made were dispersed and the bride followed the fortunes of her first lover."

It will be seen from the above that I have departed from the original conclusion of the legend in making MacEuar take summary vengeance on his enemies and in sailing away with his recovered bride.

In a legend entitled *Steeping the Withies* an incident is related of a man who shoots his enemies one by one as they emerge from a house.

RESCUE.

This story is unfounded on any particular legend.

Note on the Fairies.

Of all superstitions held amongst Celtic people, that which led to belief in the existence of the fairies seems to have been the most common and the most deeply rooted. They were supposed to be beings in appearance the counterpart of mankind, except in stature which, in their case, was, as a rule, diminutive. They could at times, however, assume gigantic proportions; or, at others, appear in forms in no way to be distinguished from those of human beings. They might sometimes give assistance to mortals, but their favours were, in the end, never productive of good and might even be destructive. Their most frequent dwelling-place was underground, beneath a knoll which could always be recognised by its perpetual verdure and luxuriance of undergrowth. These habitations might be tenanted by a single family, or by a community. The race was known as the " People of Peace " (Gaelic, " sith." Pronounced " shee ") partly perhaps because of the silence in which its members moved; for they came and went noiselessly and men were unaware, by hearing, of their approach. Sometimes, however, they made a sound resembling the rustling of a silk gown, or the whistling of a sword drawn through the air. Unearthly music, too, or songs might herald their proximity. Their dress was, for the most part, of green, except in the Isle of Skye where fairy men wore red clothing. Mortals lured to their retreats were always hospitably received and offered abundance of food and drink both, apparently, most delicious. But let the guest beware how he accept that hospitality; for, if he partake, he will become insensible to the passage of time and may remain in captivity for years; indeed he may never again return to the world of men. But should the tempting delicacies be refused, sooner or later they will be discovered in reality as disgusting refuse and all the seeming grandeur as make believe.

The fairies were most frequently seen at dusk, or on wild stormy nights of mist and driving rain. They were also apt to appear when spoken of, or when a desire was expressed for their assistance. Though themselves unseen, their presence might be made known by natural phenomena of which the most common was the eddy wind. When one on a calm summer's day saw straw and dust go past in whirling column, he might be certain that the fairies were passing by, perhaps taking captive man, woman, child or animal. But the thieves could be forced to relinquish their captive if a bonnet were thrown at them with the words, "this is yours, that's mine." Or a naked knife might be hurled with the same result.

They were often unable to suckle their own children and, therefore, would steal, when they could, a human mother to act as foster-parent. For reasons less apparent, newly born infants too were liable to capture by these troublesome beings. A block of wood in place of the mother, or an infant, or mannikin (changeling) from their own race might be substituted for the stolen child. Naked steel or iron was, however, a certain protection against all fairy power, as also was oatmeal.

THE WATER HORSE.

In *Superstitions of the Scottish Highlands* mention is made of a father and three sons who capture a water-horse in the semblance of a young man who is paying court to the daughter of the house. Except that the names of the men have been borrowed and that—as in the above story—they beguiled the disguised monster into a room where, throwing him backward on a bed, they dirked him to death, the tale of " The Water-Horse " is original.

NOTE ON THE WATER HORSE.

Almost every lonely Highland loch was, at one time, supposed to be tenanted by one or more of these monsters. In appearance they could hardly be distinguished from earthly horses, except that the head of the water-horse, sometimes at least, terminated in a flat and slippery snout. Their colour was gray or black and their manes and tails were long and flowing. They would join farm horses and their true character was so difficult to detect that the farmer was often deceived to the belief that he had acquired a valuable possession. Particularly was this the case if a cow-shackle had been thrown around the creature's neck ; for, so long as that harness was there, the captive was perfectly docile. It proved to be the best horse the farmer had and appropriately led a team when traced together. But one day the shackle is allowed to slip off, and immediately the whole team is dragged by the leader to the loch in which all disappear.

Or a stray horse is found by a pedestrian, who, without difficulty, captures the animal and mounts it ; but immediately he loses all control, is powerless even to dismount and is rushed at breathless speed to the loch into which he is plunged, never to be seen again.

The monster could assume human form and would then appear as a young man, handsome and seductive to all women towards whom he was most amorous. But let them yield to his allurements, and the waters of the loch receive them too. They might, however, detect the truth concerning the wooer, before fate overtook them, by observing that he had hoofs instead of feet and that sand and water-weeds were intermingled with his hair.

The water-horse devoured his victims with the exception of the liver, for which he, not otherwise fastidious, seemed to have had some distaste and which only would be recovered from the shore.

AN ECHO FROM THE PAST.

THOUGH the scene of this story is laid in the Highlands, some of the incidents mentioned in it in reality occurred near the ruined Castle of Henderland in Selkirkshire. The beautiful ballad of " The Border Widow's Lament " is supposed to have been sung by the widow of Pierce Cockburn, Laird of Henderland, after the execution of her husband by King James V. of Scotland. A ravine close to the ruins, through which runs a burn, is still called " The Dow Glen," or Glen of Sorrow, and a ledge of rock to this day is known as " The Lady's Seat," marking, as it is supposed to do, the spot to which the unhappy woman fled as she sought in the roar of the torrent to drown the yells which accompanied the death of her husband and his men.

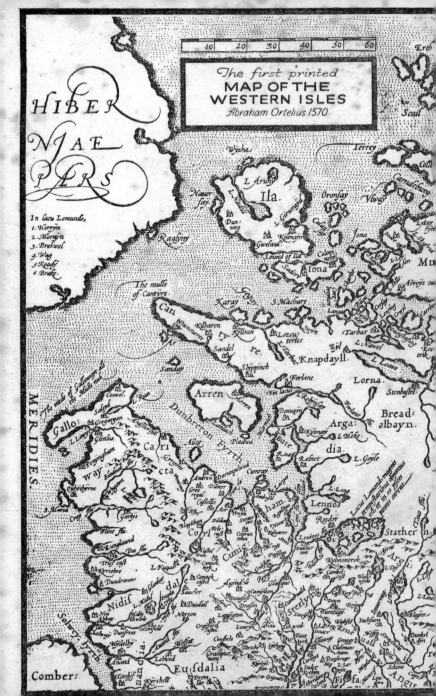